Orson Scott Card is one of the world's most popular science fiction and fantasy writers. In addition to the Ender saga, he is the author of *The Tales of Alvin Maker* and the *Homecoming* series, as well as many other stand-alone novels. He lives in Greensboro, North Carolina.

Find out more about Orson Scott Card and other Orbit authors by registering for the free monthly newsletter at www.orbitbooks.co.uk

FIRST MEETINGS

in the Enderverse

Orson Scott Card

www.orbitbooks.co.uk

An *Orbit* Book

First published in Great Britain by Orbit, 2003

Copyright © Orson Scott Card 2003

The Polish Boy
First published in *First Meetings: Three Stories from the Enderverse*
Copyright © Orson Scott Card 2002

Teacher's Pest
Published here for the first time
Copyright © Orson Scott Card 2003

Ender's Game
First published in *Analog* magazine
Copyright © Orson Scott Card 1977

Investment Counselor
First published in *Far Horizons*, edited by Robert Silverberg
Copyright © Orson Scott Card 2000

The moral right of the author has been asserted.

A CIP catalogue record for this book is available from the British Library.

ISBN 1 84149 311 2

Typeset in Garamond by M Rules
Printed and bound in Great Britain by
Mackays of Chatham plc

Orbit
An imprint of
Time Warner Books UK
Brettenham House
Lancaster Place
London WC2E 7EN

To Eugene England and Richard Cracroft,
two shepherds of LDS literature,
with respect and gratitude,
from one of the sheep

CONTENTS

THE POLISH BOY

JOHN PAUL HATED SCHOOL. HIS MOTHER DID HER BEST, but how could she possibly teach anything to him when she had eight other children – six of them to teach, two of them to tend because they were mere babies?

What John Paul hated most was the way she kept teaching him things he already knew. She would assign him to make his letters, practicing them over and over while she taught interesting things to the older kids. So John Paul did his best to make sense of the jumble of information he caught from her conversations with them. Smatterings of geography – he learned the names of dozens of nations and their capitals but wasn't quite sure what a nation was. Bits of mathematics – she taught polynomials over and over to Anna because she didn't even seem to try to understand, but it enabled John Paul to learn the operation. But he learned it like a machine, having no notion what it actually meant.

Nor could he ask. When he tried, Mother would get impatient and tell him that he would learn these things in due time, but he should concentrate on his own lessons now.

His own lessons? He wasn't getting any lessons, just boring tasks that almost made him crazy with impatience. Didn't she realize that he could already read and write as well as any of his older siblings? She made him recite from a primer, when he was perfectly capable of reading any book in the house. He tried to tell her, "I can read *that* one, Mother." But she only answered, "John Paul, that's playing. I want you to learn *real* reading."

Maybe if he didn't turn the pages of the grown-up books so quickly, she would realize that he was actually reading. But when he was interested in a book, he couldn't bear to slow down just to impress Mother. What did his reading have to do with her? It was his own. The only part of school that he enjoyed.

"You're never going to stay up with your lessons," she said more than once, "if you keep spending your reading time with these big books. Look, they don't even have pictures, why do you insist on playing with them?"

"He's not playing," said Andrew, who was twelve. "He's reading."

"Yes, yes, I should be more patient and play along," said Mother, "but I don't have time to . . ." And then one of the babies cried and the conversation was over.

Outside on the street, other children walked to

school wearing school uniforms, laughing and jostling each other. Andrew explained it to him. "They go to school in a big building. Hundreds of them in the same school."

John Paul was aghast. "Why don't their own mothers teach them? How can they learn anything with *hundreds*?"

"There's more than one teacher, silly. A teacher for every ten or fifteen of them. But they're all the same age, all learning the same thing in each class. So the teacher spends the whole day on their lessons instead of having to go from age to age."

John Paul thought a moment. "And every age has its own teacher?"

"And the teachers don't have to feed babies and change their diapers. They have time to really teach."

But what good would that have done for John Paul? They would have put him in a class with other five-year-olds and made him read stupid primers all day – and he wouldn't be able to listen to the teacher giving lessons to the ten- and twelve- and fourteen-year-olds, so he really would lose his mind.

"It's like heaven," said Andrew bitterly. "And if Father and Mother had had only two children, they could have gone there. But the minute Anna was born, we were cited for noncompliance."

John Paul was tired of hearing that word without understanding it. "What is noncompliance?"

"There's this great big war out in space," said Andrew. "Way above the sky."

"I know what space is," said John Paul impatiently.

"OK, well, big war and all, so all the countries of the world have to work together and pay to build hundreds and hundreds of starships, so they put somebody called the Hegemon in charge of the whole world. And the Hegemon says we can't afford the problems caused by overpopulation, so any marriage that has more than two children is noncompliant."

Andrew stopped as if he thought that made everything clear.

"But lots of families have more than two kids," said John Paul. Half their neighbors did.

"Because this is Poland," said Andrew, "and we're Catholic."

"What, does the priest give people extra babies?" John Paul couldn't see the connection.

"Catholics believe you should have as many children as God sends you. And no government has the right to tell you to reject God's gifts."

"What gifts?" said John Paul.

"You, dummy," said Andrew. "You're God's gift number seven in this house. And the babies are gift eight and gift nine."

"But what does it have to do with going to school?"

Andrew rolled his eyes. "You really *are* dumb," he said. "Schools are run by the government. The government has to enforce sanctions against noncompliance. And one of the sanctions is, only the first two children in a family have a right to go to school."

"But Peter and Catherine don't go to school," said John Paul.

"Because Father and Mother don't want them to learn all the anti-Catholic things the schools teach."

John Paul wanted to ask what "anti-Catholic" meant, but then he realized it must mean something like against-the-Catholics so it wasn't worth asking and having Andrew call him a dummy again.

Instead he thought and thought about it. How a war made it so all the nations gave power to one man, and that one man then told everybody how many children they could have, and all the extra children were kept out of school. That was actually a benefit, wasn't it? Not to go to school? How would John Paul have learned *anything*, if he hadn't been in the same room with Anna and Andrew and Peter and Catherine and Nicholas and Thomas, overhearing their lessons?

The most puzzling thing was the idea that the schools could teach anti-Catholic stuff. "Everybody's Catholic, aren't they?" he asked Father once.

"In Poland, yes. Or they say they are. And it used

to be true." Father's eyes were closed. His eyes were almost always closed, whenever he sat down. Even when he was eating, he always looked as though he were about to fall over and sleep. That was because he worked two jobs, the legal one during the day and the illegal one at night. John Paul almost never saw him except in the morning, and then Father was too tired to talk and Mother would shush him.

She shushed him now, even though Father had already answered him. "Don't pester your father with questions, he has important things on his mind."

"I have nothing on my mind," said Father wearily. "I have no mind."

"Anyway," said Mother.

But John Paul had another question, and he had to ask it. "If everybody's Catholic, why do the schools teach anti-Catholic?"

Father looked at him like he was crazy. "How old are you?"

He must not have understood what John Paul was asking, since it had nothing to do with ages. "I'm five, Father, don't you remember? But why do the schools teach anti-Catholic?"

Father turned to Mother. "He's only five, why are you teaching him this?"

"You taught him," said Mother. "Always ranting about the government."

"It's not our government, it's a military

occupation. Just one more attempt to extinguish Poland."

"Yes, keep talking, that's how you'll get cited again and you'll lose your job and then what will we do?"

It was obvious John Paul wasn't going to get any answer and he gave up, saving the question for later, when he got more information and could connect it together.

That was how life went on, the year John Paul was five: Mother working constantly, cooking meals and tending the babies even while she tried to run a school in the parlor, Father going away to work so early in the morning that the sun wasn't even up, and all of the children awake so they could see their father at least once a day.

Until the day Father stayed home from work.

Mother and Father were both very quiet and tense at breakfast, and when Anna asked them why Father wasn't dressed for work, Mother only snapped, "He's not going today," in a tone that said, "Ask no more questions."

With two teachers, lessons should have gone better that day. But Father was an impatient teacher, and he made Anna and Catherine so upset they fled to their rooms, and he ended up going out into the garden to weed.

So when the knock came on the door, Mother had

to send Andrew running out back to get Father. Moments later, Father came in, still brushing dirt from his hands. The knock had come twice more while he was coming, each time more insistent.

Father opened the door and stood in the frame, his large strong body filling the space. "What do you want?" he demanded. He said it in Common rather than Polish, so they knew it was a foreigner at the door.

The answer was quiet, but John Paul heard it clearly. It was a woman's voice, and she said, "I'm from the International Fleet's testing program. I understand you have three boys between the ages of six and twelve."

"Our children are none of your business."

"Actually, Mr. Wieczorek, the mandatory testing initiative is the law, and I'm here to fulfill my responsibilities under that law. If you prefer, I can have the military police come and explain it to you." She said it so mildly that John Paul almost missed the fact that it wasn't an offer she was making, it was a threat.

Father stepped back, his face grim. "What would you do, put me in jail? You've passed laws that forbid my wife from working, we have to teach our children at home, and now you'd deprive my family of any food at all."

"I don't make government policy," said the woman as she surveyed the room full of children. "All I care about is testing children."

Andrew spoke up. "Peter and Catherine already passed the government tests," he said. "Only a month ago. They're up to grade."

"This isn't about being up to grade," said the woman. "I'm not from the schools or the Polish government —"

"There is no Polish government," said Father. "Only an occupying army to enforce the dictatorship of the Hegemony."

"I'm from the fleet," said the woman. "By law we're forbidden even to express opinions of Hegemony policy while we're in uniform. The sooner I begin the testing, the sooner you can go back to your regular routines. They all speak Common?"

"Of course," said Mother, a little pridefully. "At least as well as they speak Polish."

"I watch the test," said Father.

"I'm sorry, sir," said the woman, "but you do not watch. You provide me with a room where I can be alone with each child, and if you have only one room in your dwelling, you take everyone outside or to a neighbor's house. I *will* conduct these tests."

Father tried to face her down, but he had no weapons for this battle, and he looked away. "It doesn't matter if you test or not. Even if they pass, I'm not letting you take them."

"Let's cross that bridge when we come to it," said the woman. She looked sad. And John Paul suddenly understood why: Because she knew that Father would have no choice about anything, but she didn't want to embarrass him by pointing it out. She just wanted to do her job and go.

John Paul didn't know how he knew these things, but sometimes they just came to him. It wasn't like history facts or geography or mathematics, where you had to learn things before you knew them. He could just look at people and listen to them and suddenly he'd know things about them. About what they wanted or why they were doing the things they were doing. When his brothers and sisters quarreled, for instance. He usually got a clear idea of just what was causing the quarrel, and most of the time he knew, without even trying to think of it, just the right thing to say to make the quarreling stop. Sometimes he didn't say it, because he didn't mind if they quarreled. But when one of them was getting really angry – angry enough to hit – then John Paul would say the thing he needed to say, and the fight would stop, just like that.

With Peter, it was often something like, "Just do what he says, Peter's the boss of everybody," and then Peter's face would turn red and he'd leave the room and the argument would stop, just like that. Because Peter hated having people say he thought he was boss. But that didn't work with Anna, with her it took something like, "Your face is getting all red," and then John Paul would laugh, and she would go outside and screech and then come back inside and storm around the house, but the quarrel itself was over. Because Anna hated to think she ever, ever looked funny or silly.

And even now, he knew that if he just said, "Papa, I'm scared," Father would push the woman out of the house and then he would be in so much trouble. But if John Paul said, "Papa, can I take the test, too?" Father would laugh and he wouldn't look so ashamed and unhappy and angry.

So he said it.

Father laughed. "That's John Paul, always wants to do more than he's able."

The woman looked at John Paul. "How old is he?"

"Not six yet," said Mother sharply.

"Oh," said the woman. "Well, then, I assume this is Nicholas, this is Thomas, and this is Andrew?"

"Why aren't you testing me?" demanded Peter.

"I'm afraid you're already too old," she answered. "By the time the Fleet was able to gain access to non-compliant nations . . ." Her voice trailed off.

Peter got up and mournfully left the room.

"Why not girls?" said Catherine.

"Because girls don't want to be soldiers," said Anna.

And suddenly John Paul realized that this wasn't like the regular government tests. This was a test that Peter *wanted* to take, and Catherine was jealous that it couldn't be given to girls.

If this test was about becoming a soldier, it was dumb that Peter would be considered too old. He was the only one who had his man-height. What, did they think Andrew or Nicholas could carry a gun and kill people? Maybe Thomas could, but he was also kind of fat besides being tall and he didn't look like any soldier John Paul had seen.

"Whom do you want first?" asked Mother. "And can you do it in a bedroom so I can keep their lessons going?"

"Regulations require that I do it in a room with street access, with the door open," said the woman.

"Oh, for the love of – we aren't going to hurt you," said Father.

The woman only looked at him briefly, and then looked at Mother, and both of John Paul's parents seemed to give in. John Paul realized: Somebody must have been hurt giving this test. Somebody must have been taken into a back room and somebody hurt them. Or killed them. This was a dangerous business. Some people must be even angrier about the testing than Father and Mother.

Why would Father and Mother hate and fear something that Peter and Catherine wished they could have?

*

It proved impossible to have a regular school day in the girls' bedroom, even though it had the fewest beds, and soon Mother resorted to having a free-reading time while she nursed one of the babies.

And when John Paul asked if he could go read in the other room, she gave consent.

Of course, she assumed he meant the other bedroom, because whenever somebody in the family said "the other room" they meant the other bedroom. But John Paul had no intention of going in there. Instead he headed for the kitchen.

Father and Mother had forbidden the children to enter the parlor while the testing was going on, but that didn't prevent John Paul from sitting on the floor just outside the parlor, reading a book while he listened to the test.

Every now and then he was aware that the woman giving the test was glancing at him, but she never said anything to him and so he just kept reading. It was a book about the life of St. John Paul II, the great Polish pope that he had been named for, and John Paul was fascinated because he was finally getting answers to some of his questions about why Catholics were different and the Hegemon didn't like them.

Even as he read, he also listened to all of the testing. But it wasn't like the government tests, with questions about facts and seeing if they could figure out math answers or name parts of speech. Instead she asked each boy questions that didn't really have answers. About what he liked and didn't like, about why people did the things they did. Only after about fifteen minutes of those questions did she start the written test with more regular problems.

In fact, the first time, John Paul didn't think those questions were part of the test. Only when she asked each boy the exact same questions and then followed up on the differences in their answers did he realize this was definitely one of the main things she was here to do. And from the way she got so involved and tense asking those questions, John Paul gathered that she thought these questions were actually more important than the written part of the test.

John Paul wanted to answer the questions. He wanted to take the test. He liked to take tests. He always answered silently when the older children were taking tests, to see if he could answer as many questions as they did.

So when she was finishing up with Andrew, John Paul was just about to ask if he could take the test when the woman spoke to Mother. "How old is this one?"

"We told you," said Mother. "He's only five."

"Look what he's reading."

"He just turns the pages. It's a game. He's imitating the way he sees the older children read."

"He's reading," said the woman.

"Oh, you're here for a few hours and you know more about my children than I do, even though I teach them for hours every day?"

The woman did not argue. "What is his name?"

Mother didn't want to answer.

"John Paul," said John Paul.

Mother glared at him. So did Andrew.

"I want to take the test," he said.

"You're too young," said Andrew, in Polish.

"I turn six in three weeks," said John Paul. He spoke in Common. He wanted the woman to understand him.

The woman nodded. "I'm allowed to test him early," she said.

"Allowed, but not required," said Father, coming into the room. "What's he doing in here?"

"He said he was going into the other room to read," said Mother. "I thought he meant the other bedroom."

"I'm in the kitchen," said John Paul.

"He didn't disturb anything," said the woman.

"Too bad," said Father.

"I'd like to test him," the woman said.

"No," said Father.

"Somebody will just have to come back in three weeks and do it then," she said. "And disrupt your day one more time. Why not have done with it today?"

"He's already heard the answers," said Mother. "If he was sitting here listening."

"The test isn't like that," said the woman. "It's all right that he heard."

John Paul could see already that Father and Mother were both going to give in, so he didn't bother saying anything to try to influence them. He didn't want to use his ability to say the right words too often, or somebody would catch on, and it would stop working.

It took a few more minutes of conversation, but then John Paul was sitting on the couch beside the woman.

"I really was reading," said John Paul.

"I know," said the woman.

"How?" asked John Paul.

"Because you were turning the pages in a regular rhythm," she said. "You read very fast, don't you?"

John Paul nodded. "When it's interesting."

"And St. John Paul II is an interesting man?"

"He did what he thought was right," said John Paul.

"You're named after him," she said.

"He was very brave," said John Paul. "And he never did what bad people wanted him to do, if he thought it was important."

"What bad people?"

"The Communists," said John Paul.

"How do you know they were bad people? Does the book say so?"

Not in words, John Paul realized. "They were making people do things. They were trying to punish people for being Catholic."

"And that's bad?"

"God is Catholic," said John Paul.

The woman smiled. "Muslims think that God is a Muslim."

John Paul digested this. "Some people think God doesn't exist."

"That's true," said the woman.

"Which?" he asked.

She chuckled. "That some people think he doesn't exist. I don't know, myself. I don't have an opinion on the subject."

"That means you don't believe there is a God," said John Paul.

"Oh, does it?"

"St. John Paul II said so. That saying you don't know or care about God is the same as saying you believe he doesn't exist, because if you had even a hope that he existed, you would care very much."

She laughed. "Just turning the pages, were you?"

"I can answer all your questions," he said.

"Before I ask them?"

"I wouldn't hit him," said John Paul, answering the question about what he would do if a friend tried to take away something of his. "Because then he wouldn't be my friend. But I wouldn't let him take the thing either."

The follow-up to this answer had been, How would you stop him? So John Paul went right on without pausing. "The way I'd stop him is, I'd say, 'You can have it. I give it to you, it's yours now. Because I'd rather keep you as a friend than keep that thing.'"

"Where did you learn that?" asked the woman.

"That's not one of the questions," said John Paul.

She shook her head. "No, it's not."

"I think sometimes you have to hurt people," said John Paul, answering the next question, which had been, Is there ever a time when you have a right to hurt somebody else?

He answered every question, including the follow-ups, without her having to ask any of them. He did it in the same order she had asked them of his brothers, and when he was done, he said, "Now the written part. I don't know those questions cause I couldn't see them and you didn't say them."

They were easier than he thought. They were about shapes and remembering things and picking out right sentences and doing numbers, things like that. She kept looking at her watch, so he hurried.

When it was all done, she just sat there looking at him.

"Did I do it right?" asked John Paul.

She nodded.

He studied her face, the way she sat, the way her hands didn't move, the way she looked at him. The way she was breathing. He realized that she was very excited, trying hard to stay calm. That's why she wasn't speaking. She didn't want him to know.

But he knew.

He was what she had come here looking for.

"Some people might say that this is why women can't be used for testing," said Col. Sillain.

"Then those people would be mentally deficient," said Helena Rudolf.

"Too susceptible to a cute face," said Sillain. "Too prone to go 'Aw' and give a kid the benefit of the doubt on everything."

"Fortunately, you don't harbor any such suspicions," said Helena.

"No," said Sillain. "That's because I happen to know you have no heart."

"There we are," said Helena. "We finally understand each other."

"And you say this Polish five-year-old is more than just precocious."

"Heaven knows, that's the main thing our tests identify – general precociousness."

"There are better tests being developed. Very

specific for military ability. And younger than you might think."

"Too bad that it's already almost too late."

Col. Sillain shrugged. "There's a theory that we don't actually have to put them through a full course of training."

"Yes, yes, I read all about how young Alexander was. It helped that he was the son of the king and that he fought unmotivated armies of mercenaries."

"So you think the Buggers are motivated."

"The Buggers are a commander's dream," said Helena. "They don't question orders, they just *do*. Whatever."

"Also a commander's nightmare," said Sillain. "They don't think for themselves."

"John Paul Wieczorek is the real thing," said Helena. "And in thirty-five years, he'll be forty. So the Alexander theory won't have to be tested."

"Now you're talking as if you're sure he'll be the one."

"I don't know that," said Helena. "But he's something. The things he says."

"I read your report."

"When he said, 'I'd rather keep you as a friend than keep that thing,' I about lost it. I mean, he's five."

"And that didn't set off your alarms? He sounds coached."

"But he wasn't. His parents didn't want any of them tested, least of all him, being underage and all."

"They *said* they didn't want."

"The father stayed home from work to try to stop me."

"Or to make you *think* he wanted to stop you."

"He can't afford to lose a day's pay. Noncompliant parents don't get paid vacations."

"I know," said Sillain. "Wouldn't it be ironic if this John Paul Whatever –"

"Wieczorek."

"Yes, that's the one. Wouldn't it be ironic if, after all our stringent population control efforts – for the sake of the war, mind you – it turned out that the commander of the fleet turned out to be the seventh child of noncompliant parents?"

"Yes, very ironic."

"I think one theory was that birth order predicts that only firstborns would have the personality for what we need."

"All else being equal. Which it isn't."

"We're so ahead of ourselves here, Captain Rudolf," said Sillain. "The parents are not likely to say yes, are they?"

"No, not likely," said Helena.

"So it's all moot, isn't it?"

"Not if . . ."

"Oh, that would be so wise, to make an international incident out of this." He leaned back in his chair.

"I don't think it would be an international incident."

"The treaty with Poland has very strict parental-control provisions. Have to respect the family and all."

"The Poles are very anxious to rejoin the rest of the world. They aren't going to invoke that clause if we impress on them how important this boy is."

"Is he?" asked Sillain. "That's the question. If he's worth the gamble of making a huge stink about it."

"If it starts to stink, we can back off," said Helena.

"Oh, I can see *you've* done a lot of public relations work."

"Come see him yourself," said Helena. "He'll be six in a few days. Come see him. Then tell me whether he's worth the risk of an international incident."

This was not at all how John Paul wanted to spend his birthday. Mother had made candy all day with sugar she begged from neighbors, and John Paul wanted to suck on his, not chew it, so it would last and last. Instead Father told him either to spit it out into the garbage or swallow it, and so now it was swallowed and gone, all for these people from the International Fleet.

"We got some questionable results from the pre-liminary screening," said the man. "Perhaps because the child had listened to three previous tests. We need to get accurate information, that's all."

He was lying – that was obvious, from the way he moved, the way he looked Father right in the eye, unwaveringly. A liar who knew he was lying and was trying hard not to look like he was lying. The way Thomas always did. It fooled Father but never Mother, and never John Paul.

So if the man was lying, why? Why was he really coming to test John Paul again?

He remembered what he had thought right after the woman tested him three weeks ago, that she had found what she was looking for. But then nothing had happened and he figured he must have been wrong. Now she was back and the man who was with her was telling lies.

The family was banished to other rooms. It was evening, time for Father to go to his second job, only he couldn't go while these people were here or they'd know, or guess, or wonder what he was doing, hour after hour during the evening. So the longer this took, the less money Father would earn tonight, and therefore the less food they'd be able to eat, the less clothing they'd have to wear.

The man even sent the woman out of the room. That annoyed John Paul. He liked the woman.

He didn't like at all the way the man looked at their house. At the other children. At Mother and Father. As if he thought himself better than they were.

The man asked a question.

John Paul answered in Polish instead of Common.

The man looked at him blankly. He called out, "I thought he spoke Common!"

The woman stuck her head back into the room. Apparently she had only gone to the kitchen. "He does, fluently," said the woman.

The man looked back at John Paul, and the disdainful look was gone. "So what game are you playing?"

In Polish, John Paul said, "The only reason we're poor is because the Hegemon punishes Catholics for obeying God."

"In Common, please," said the man.

"The language is called English," said John Paul in Polish, "and why should I talk to you at all?"

The man sighed. "Sorry to waste your time." He got up.

The woman came back into the room. They thought they were whispering soft enough, but like most adults, they thought that children didn't understand adult conversations so they weren't all that careful about being quiet.

"He's defying you," said the woman.

"Yes, I guessed that," said the man testily.

"So if you go, he wins."

Good one, thought John Paul. This woman wasn't stupid. She knew what to say to make this man do what she wanted.

"Or somebody does."

She walked over to John Paul. "Colonel Sillain thinks I was lying when I said you did so well on the tests."

In Common, John Paul said, "How well *did* I do?"

The woman only got a little smile on her face and glanced back at Col. Sillain.

Sillain sat back down. "All right then. Are you ready?"

In Polish, John Paul said, "I'm ready if you speak Polish."

Impatiently, Sillain turned back to the woman. "What does he want?"

In Common, John Paul said to the woman, "Tell him I don't want to be tested by a man who thinks my family is scum."

"In the first place," said the man, "I don't think that."

"Liar," said John Paul in Polish.

He turned to the woman. She shrugged helplessly. "I don't speak Polish either."

John Paul said to her, in Common, "You rule over us but you don't bother to learn our language. Instead we have to learn yours."

She laughed. "It's not my language. Or his. Common is just a universalized dialect of English, and I'm German." She pointed at Sillain. "He's Finnish. Nobody speaks *his* language anymore. Not even the Finns."

"Listen," said Sillain, turning to John Paul. "I'm not going to play around anymore. You speak Common, and I don't speak Polish, so answer my questions in Common."

"What are you going to do?" asked John Paul in Polish, "put me in jail?"

It was fun watching Sillain turn redder and redder, but then Father came into the room, looking very weary. "John Paul," he said. "Do what the man asks."

"They want to take me away from you," said John Paul in Common.

"Nothing of the kind," said the man.

"He's lying," said John Paul.

The man turned slightly red.

"And he hates us. He thinks we're poor and that it's disgusting to have so many children."

"That is not true," said Sillain.

Father ignored him. "We are poor, John Paul."

"Only because of the Hegemony," said John Paul.

"Don't preach my own sermons back at me," said Father. But he switched to Polish to say it. "If you don't do what they want, then they can punish your mother and me."

Father sometimes knew exactly the right words to say, too.

John Paul turned back to Sillain. "I don't want to be alone with you. I want *her* to be here for the test."

"Part of the test," said Sillain, "is seeing how well you obey orders."

"Then I fail," said John Paul.

Both the woman and Father laughed.

Sillain did not. "It's obvious that this child has been trained to be noncooperative, Captain Rudolf. Let's go."

"He has not been trained," said Father.

John Paul could see that he looked worried.

"Nobody trained me," said John Paul.

"The mother didn't even know he could read at college level," said the woman softly.

College level? John Paul thought that was ridiculous. Once you knew the letters, reading was reading. How could there be levels?

"She wanted you to think she didn't know," said Sillain.

"My mother doesn't lie," said John Paul.

"No, no, of course not," said Sillain. "I didn't mean to imply —"

Now he was revealing the truth: That he was frightened. Afraid that John Paul might not take his test. His fear meant that John Paul had power in this situation. Even more than he had thought.

"I'll answer your questions," said John Paul, "if the lady stays here."

This time, he knew, Sillain would say yes.

They gathered with a dozen experts and military leaders in a conference room in Berlin. Everyone had already seen Col. Sillain's and Helena's reports. They had seen John Paul's test scores. They had watched the vid of Sillain's conversation with John Paul Wieczorek before, during, and after the test.

Helena enjoyed how much Sillain hated having to watch this six-year-old Polish boy manipulate him. It hadn't been so obvious at the time, of course, but after you watched the vid over and over, it became painfully obvious. And, while everyone at the table was polite, there were a few raised eyebrows, a nod, a couple of half-smiles when John Paul said, "Then I fail."

At the end of the vid, a Russian general from the office of the Strategos said, "Was he bluffing?"

"He's six," said the young Indian representing the Polemarch.

"That's what's so terrifying," said the teacher who was there for the Battle School. "About all the children at Battle School, actually. Most people live their whole lives without ever meeting a single child like this one."

"So, Captain Graff," said the Indian, "are you saying he's nothing special?"

"They're all special," said Graff. "But this one – his tests are good, top range. Not the very best we've seen, but the tests aren't as predictive as we'd like. It's his negotiating skill that impresses me."

Helena wanted to say, "Or Colonel Sillain's lack of it." But she knew that wasn't fair. Sillain had tried a bluff, and the boy had called it. Who knew a child would have the wit to do that?

"Well," said the Indian, "it certainly shows the wisdom of opening Battle School to noncompliant nations."

"There's only one problem, Captain Chamrajnagar," said Graff. "In all these documents, on this vid, in our conversation, no one has even suggested that the boy is willing to go."

There was silence around the table.

"Well, no, of course not," said Col. Sillain. "This meeting came first. There is some hostility from the parents – the father stayed home from work when Helena – Captain Rudolf went to test three of the older brothers. I think there may be trouble. We needed to assess, before the conversation, just how much leverage I'm to be given."

"You mean," said Graff, "leverage to coerce the family?"

"Or entice," said Sillain.

"Poles are stubborn people," said the Russian general. "It's in the Slavic character."

"We're so close," said Graff, "to tests that are well over ninety percent accurate in predicting military ability."

"Do you have a test to measure leadership?" asked Chamrajnagar.

"That's one of the components," said Graff.

"Because this boy has it, off the charts," said Chamrajnagar. "I've never even seen the charts, and I know that."

"The real training ground for leadership is in the game," said Graff. "But yes, I think this boy will do well at it."

"If he goes," said the Russian.

"I think," said Chamrajnagar, "that Colonel Sillain should not carry out the next step."

This left Sillain sputtering. Helena wanted to smile, but instead she said, "Colonel Sillain is the team leader, and according to protocol . . ."

"He has already been compromised," said Chamrajnagar. "I make no criticism of Colonel Sillain, please. I don't know which of us would have fared any better. But the boy made him back down, and I don't think there is a helpful relationship."

Sillain was careerist enough to know how to hand them his head, when asked for it. "Whatever is best to accomplish the mission, of course." Helena knew how he had to be seething at Chamrajnagar, but he showed no sign of it.

"The question Colonel Sillain asked still remains," said Graff. "What authority will the negotiator be given?"

"All the authority he needs," said the Russian general.

"But that's precisely what we don't know," said Graff.

Chamrajnagar answered. "I think my colleague from the Strategos's office is saying that whatever inducement the negotiator feels is appropriate will be supported by the Strategos. Certainly the Polemarch's office has the same view."

"I don't think the boy is that important," said Graff. "Battle School exists because of the need to begin military training during childhood in order to build appropriate habits of thought and movement. But there has been enough data to suggest —"

"We know this story," said the Russian general.

"Let's not begin this argument again here," said Chamrajnagar.

"There is a definite fall-off in outcomes after the trainees reach adulthood," said Graff. "That's a fact, however much we may not like the implications."

"They know more, but do worse?" said Chamrajnagar. "It sounds wrong. It is hard to believe, and even if we believe it, it is hard to interpret."

"It means that we don't have to have this boy, because we won't have to wait for a child to grow to adulthood."

The Russian general was scornful. "Put our war in the hands of children? I hope we are never that desperate."

There was a long silence, and then Chamrajnagar spoke. Apparently he had been receiving instructions through his earpiece. "The office of the Polemarch believes that because this data Captain Graff speaks of is incomplete, prudence suggests we act as if we do, in fact, have to have this boy. Time is growing short, and it is impossible to know whether he might be our last best chance."

"The Stratego concurs," said the Russian general.

"Yes," said Graff. "As I said, the results are not final."

"So, said Col. Sillain. "Full authority. For whoever it is who negotiates."

"I think," said Chamrajnagar, "that the director of Battle School has already demonstrated whom he has the most confidence in right now, planetside."

All eyes went to Capt. Graff. "I would be glad to have Captain Rudolf accompany me. I believe we have it on record that this Polish boy prefers to have her present."

This time when the Fleet people came, Father and Mother were prepared. Their friend Magda was a lawyer, and even though she was forbidden, as a non-compliant, to practice law, she sat between them on the sofa.

John Paul was not in the room, however. "Don't let them bully the child," Magda had said, and that was it. Mother and Father immediately banned him from the room, so he didn't even get to see them come in.

He could listen, however, from the kitchen. He realized at once that the man he didn't like, the colonel, was not there, though the woman was. A new man was with her now. His voice didn't have the sound of lying in it. Captain Graff, he was called.

After the polite things were said – the sitting down, the offering of drinks – Graff got down to business quickly. "I see that you do not wish me to see the child."

Magda answered, quite imperiously, "His parents felt it best for him not to be present."

Silence for a long moment.

"Magdalena Teczlo," said Graff softly, "these good people may invite a friend over to sit with them today. But I'd hate to think you might be acting as their attorney."

If Magda answered, John Paul couldn't hear.

"I would like to see the boy now," said Graff.

Father started explaining that that would never happen, so if that's all he wanted, he might as well give up and go home.

Another long silence. There was no sound of Captain Graff getting up from the chair, an operation that could not be performed silently. So he must be sitting there, saying nothing – not leaving, but not trying to persuade them.

That was a shame, because John Paul wanted to see what he would say to get them to do what he wanted. The way he silenced Magda was intriguing. John Paul wanted to see what was happening. He stepped from behind the dividing wall and watched.

Graff was doing nothing. There was no threat on his face, no attempt to outface them. He gazed pleasantly at Mother, and then at Father, and then at Mother again, skipping right over Magda's face. It was as if she didn't exist – even her own body seemed to say, "Don't notice me, I'm not really here."

Graff turned his head and looked right at John Paul.

John Paul thought he might say something to get him in trouble, but Graff gazed at him only a moment and then turned back to Mother and Father. "You understand, of course," he began.

"No, I don't understand," said Father. "You aren't going to see the boy unless we decide you'll see him, and for that you have to meet our terms."

Graff looked blandly back at him. "He isn't your breadwinner. What possible hardship can you claim?"

"We don't want a handout," said Father furiously. "We aren't looking for compensation."

"All I want," said Graff, "is to converse with the boy."

"Not alone," said Father.

"With us here," said Mother.

"That's fine with me," said Graff. "But I think Magdalena is sitting in the boy's place."

Magda, after a moment's hesitation, got up and left the house. The door banged shut just a little louder than usual.

Graff beckoned to John Paul.

He came in and sat on the couch between his parents.

Graff began to explain to him about Battle School. That he would go up into space in order to study how to be a soldier so he could help fight against the Buggers when they came back with the next invasion. "You might lead fleets into battle someday," said Graff. "Or lead marines as they blast their way through an enemy ship."

"I can't go," said John Paul.

"Why not?" asked Graff.

"I'd miss my lessons," he said. "My mother teaches us, here in this room."

Graff didn't answer, just studied John Paul's face. It made John Paul uncomfortable.

The Fleet lady spoke up. "But you'll have teachers there. In Battle School."

John Paul did not look at her. It was Graff he had

to watch. Graff was the one with all the power today.

Finally Graff spoke. "You think it would be unfair for you to be in Battle School while your family still struggles here."

John Paul had not thought of that. But now that Graff had suggested it . . .

"Nine of us," said John Paul. "It's very hard for my mother to teach us all at once."

"What if the Fleet can persuade the government of Poland –"

"Poland has no government," said John Paul, and then he smiled up at his father, who beamed down at him.

"The current rulers of Poland," said Graff cheerfully enough. "What if we can persuade them to lift the sanctions on your brothers and sisters."

John Paul thought about this for a moment. He tried to imagine what it would be like, if they could all go to school. Easier for Mother. That would be good.

He looked up at his father.

Father blinked. John Paul knew that face. Father was trying to keep from showing that he was disappointed. So there was something wrong.

Of course. There were sanctions on Father, too. Andrew had explained to him once that Father wasn't allowed to work at his real job, which should have been teaching at a university. Instead Father had to do a clerical job all day, sitting at a computer, and then manual labor by night, odd jobs off the books in the Catholic underground. If they would lift the sanctions on the children, why not on the parents?

"Why can't they change all the stupid rules?" said John Paul.

Graff looked at Capt. Rudolf, then at John Paul's parents. "Even if we could," he said to them, "should we?"

Mother rubbed John Paul's back a little. "John Paul means well, but of course we can't. Not even the sanctions against the children's schooling."

John Paul was instantly furious. What did she mean, "of course?" If they had only bothered to explain things to him then he wouldn't be making mistakes, but no, even after these people from the Fleet came to prove that John Paul wasn't just a stupid kid, they treated him like a stupid kid.

But he did not show his anger. That never got good results from Father, and it made Mother anxious so she didn't think well.

The only answer he made was to say, with wide-eyed innocence, "Why not?"

"You'll understand when you're older," said Mother.

He wanted to say, "And when will you understand anything about me? Even after you realized I could read, you still think I don't know anything."

But then, he apparently didn't know everything he needed to, or he'd see what was obvious to all these adults.

If his parents wouldn't tell him, maybe this captain would.

John Paul looked expectantly at Graff.

And Graff gave the explanation he needed.

"All of your parents' friends are noncompliant Catholics. If your brothers and sisters suddenly get to go to school, if your father suddenly gets to go back to the university, what will they think?"

So this was about the neighborhood. John Paul could hardly believe that his parents would sacrifice their children, even themselves, just so the neighbors wouldn't resent them.

"We could move," said John Paul.

"Where?" asked Father. "There are noncompliants like us, and there are people who gave up their faith. There's only the two groups, and I'd rather go on as we are than to cross that line. It's not about the neighbors, John Paul. It's about our own integrity. It's about faith."

It wasn't going to work, John Paul could see that now. He had thought that his Battle School idea could be turned to help his family. He would have gone into space for that, gone away and not come home for years, if it would have helped his family.

"You can still come," said Graff. "Even if your

family doesn't want to be free of these sanctions."

Father erupted then, not shouting, but his voice hot and intense. "We want to be free of the sanctions, you fool. We just don't want to be the only ones free of them! We want the Hegemony to stop telling Catholics they have to commit mortal sin, to repudiate the Church. We want the Hegemony to stop forcing Poles to act like . . . like *Germans*."

But John Paul knew this rant, and knew that his father usually ended that sentence by saying, "forcing Poles to act like Jews and atheists and Germans." The omission told him that Father did not want the results that would come from talking in front of these Fleet people the way he talked in front of other Poles. John Paul had read enough history to know why. And it occurred to him that even though Father suffered greatly under the sanctions, maybe in his anger and resentment he had become a man who no longer belonged at the university. Father knew another set of rules and chose not to live by them. But Father also did not want educated foreigners to know that he did not live by those rules. He did not want them to know that he blamed things on Jews and atheists. But to blame them on Germans, that was all right.

Suddenly John Paul wanted nothing more than to leave home. To go to a school where he wouldn't have to listen in on someone else's lessons.

The only problem was, John Paul had no interest

in war. When he read history, he skimmed those parts. And yet it was called Battle School. He would have to study war a lot, he was sure of it. And in the end, if he didn't fail, he would have to serve in the Fleet. Take orders from men and women like these Fleet officers. To do other people's bidding all his life.

He was only six, but he already knew that he hated it when he had to do what other people wanted, even when he knew that they were wrong. He didn't want to be a soldier. He didn't want to kill. He didn't want to die. He didn't want to obey stupid people.

At the same time, he didn't want to stay in this situation, either. Crowded into their apartment most of the day. Mother always so tired. None of them learning all they could. Never quite enough to eat, nothing but shabby threadbare clothing, never warm enough in winter, always sweltering in summer.

They all think we're being heroes, like St. John Paul II under the Nazis and the Communists. Standing up for the faith against the lies and evils of the world, the way St. John Paul II did as pope.

But what if we're just being stubborn and stupid? What if everybody else is right, and we shouldn't have had more than two children in our family?

Then I wouldn't have been born.

Am I really here because God wants me to be? Maybe God wanted all kinds of children to be born, and all the rest of the world was blocking them from coming by their sins, because of the Hegemon's laws. Maybe it was like the story of Abraham and Sodom, where God would be willing to save the city from destructions if twenty righteous people could be found, or even ten. Maybe we're the righteous people who save the world just by existing, just by serving God and refusing to bow to the Hegemon.

But existing is not all I want, thought John Paul. I want to do something. I want to learn everything and know everything and do every good thing. To have choices. And I want my brothers and sisters to have those choices too. I will never have power like this again, to change the world around me. The moment these people from the Fleet decide they don't want me anymore, I'll never have another chance. I have to do something now.

"I don't want to stay here," said John Paul.

He could feel Father's body stiffen on the couch next to him, and Mother gasped just the tiniest of gasps inside her throat.

"But I don't want to go into space," said John Paul.

Graff did not move. But he blinked.

"I've never been to a school. I don't know if I'll like it," said John Paul. "Everybody I know is Polish and Catholic. I don't know what it's like to be with people who aren't."

"If you don't go into the Battle School program," said Graff, "there's nothing we can do about the rest."

"Can't we go somewhere and try it out?" asked John Paul. "Can't we all go somewhere that we can go to school and nobody will care that we're Catholics and there are nine of us children?"

"There's nowhere in the world like that," said Father bitterly.

John Paul looked at Graff questioningly.

"Your father is partly right," said Graff. "A family with nine children will always be resented, no matter where you go. And here, because there are so many other noncompliant families, you sustain each other. There's solidarity. In some ways it would be worse if you left Poland."

"In every way," said Father.

"But we could set you up in a large city, and then send no more than two of your brothers and sisters to any one school. That way, if they are careful, no one will know that their family is noncompliant."

"If they become liars, you mean," said Mother.

"Oh," said Graff, "forgive me. I didn't know that your family never, ever told a lie to protect your family's interests."

"You're trying to seduce us," said Mother. "To divide the family. To get our children into schools that will teach them to deny the faith, to despise the Church."

"Ma'am," said Graff, "I'm trying to get a very promising boy to agree to come to Battle School because the world faces a terrible enemy."

"Does it?" said Mother. "I keep hearing about this terrible enemy, these Buggers, these monsters from space, but where are they?"

"The reason you don't see them," said Graff patiently, "is because we defeated their first two invasions. And if you ever do see them, it will be because we lost the third time. And even then you won't see them, because they will do such terrible things to the surface of the Earth that there will be no humans alive when the first of the Buggers sets foot here. We want your son to help us prevent that."

"If God sends these monsters to kill us, maybe it's as it was in the days of Noah," said Mother. "Maybe the world is so wicked it needs to be destroyed."

"Well, if that's so," said Graff, "then we'll lose the war, no matter what we do, and that's that. But what if God wants us to win, so we have more time to repent of our wickedness? Don't you think we ought to leave that possibility open?"

"Don't argue theology with us," said Father coldly, "as if you were a believer."

"You don't know what I believe," said Graff. "All you know is this: We will go to great lengths to get your son into Battle School, because we believe he is extraordinary, and we believe that in this house he has been and will continue to be frustrated. Wasted."

But why? What was Graff trying to accomplish?

Then he realized: Graff wanted to show John Paul this scene. Father humiliated, beaten down, and Mother reduced to weeping over him.

Graff spoke, as he gazed intensely into John Paul's eyes. "The war is a desperate struggle, John Paul. They nearly broke us. They nearly won. It was only because we had a genius, a commander named Mazer Rackham who was able to outguess them, to find their weaknesses, that we barely, barely won. Who will be that commander next time? Will he be there? Or will he still be somewhere in Poland, working two miserable jobs that are far beneath his intellectual ability, all because at the age of six he thought he didn't *want* to go into space."

Ah. That was it. The captain wanted John Paul to see what defeat looked like.

But I already know what defeat looks like. And I'm not going to let you defeat me.

"There are still Catholics outside Poland?" asked John Paul. "Noncompliant ones, right?"

"Yes," said Graff.

"But not every nation is ruled by the Hegemony the way Poland is."

"Compliant nations continue to be governed by their traditional system."

"So is there some nation where we could be with other noncompliant Catholics, and yet still not have such bad sanctions that we can't even get enough food to eat, and Father can't work?"

"Compliant nations all have to have sanctions against overpopulators," said Graff. "That's what being compliant means."

"A nation," said John Paul, "where we could be an exception, and nobody would have to know it?"

"Canada," said Graff. "New Zealand. Sweden. America. Noncompliants who don't make speeches about it get along decently there. You wouldn't be the only ones who had children going to different schools, with the authorities looking the other way, because they hate punishing children for the sins of the parents."

"Which is best?" asked John Paul. "Which has the most Catholics?"

"America. The most Poles *and* the most Catholics. And Americans always think international laws are for other people anyway, so they don't take Hegemony rules quite as seriously."

"Could we go there?" asked John Paul.

"No," said Father. He was sitting up now, his head still bowed in pain and humiliation.

"John Paul," said Graff, "we don't want you to go to America. We want you to go to Battle School."

"I won't go unless my family is in a place where we

won't be hungry and where my brothers and sisters can go to school. I'll just stay here."

"He's not going anyway," said Father, "no matter what you say, no matter what you promise, no matter what John Paul decides."

"Oh, yes, *you*," said Graff. "You just committed the felony of striking an officer of the International Fleet, for which the penalty is imprisonment for a term of not less than three years – but you know how the courts put much heavier penalties on noncompliants who are convicted of crime. My guess would be seven or eight years. It's all recorded, of course, the entire thing."

"You came into our house as a spy," said Mother. "You provoked him."

"I spoke the truth to you, and you didn't like hearing it," said Graff. "I did not raise a hand against Professor Wieczorek or anyone in your family."

"Please," said Father. "Don't send me to jail."

"Of course I won't," said Graff. "I don't want you in jail. But I also don't want you issuing foolish declarations of what will or will not happen, no matter what I say, no matter what I promise, no matter what John Paul decides."

This was why Graff had goaded Father, John Paul understood now. To make sure Father had no choice but to go along with whatever John Paul and Graff decided between them.

"What are you going to do to me to make me do what you want," said John Paul, "the way you did with Father?"

"It won't do me any good," said Graff, "if you come with me unwillingly."

"I won't come with you willingly unless my family is in a place where they can be happy."

"There is no such place in a world ruled by the Hegemony," said Father.

But now it was Mother who stopped Father from speaking more. With a gentle hand she touched his face. "We can be good Catholics in another place," she said. "For us to leave here, that doesn't take bread out of the mouths of our neighbors. It harms no one. Look what John Paul is trying to do for us." She turned to John Paul. "I'm sorry I didn't know the truth about you. I'm sorry I was such a bad teacher for you." Then she burst into tears.

Father put his arm around her, pulled her close, rocked her, the two of them sitting on the floor, comforting each other.

Graff looked at John Paul, eyebrows raised, as if to say, I've removed all the obstacles, so . . . do what I want.

But things weren't yet the way John Paul wanted them.

"You'll cheat me," said John Paul. "You'll take us to America but then if I still decide not to go, you'll threaten to send everybody back here, worse off than before, and that's how you'll force me to go."

Graff did not answer for a moment.

"So I won't go," said John Paul.

"You'll cheat *me*," said Graff. "You'll get me to move your family to America and set you up in a better life, and then you'll refuse to go anyway, and you'll expect the International Fleet to allow your family to continue to enjoy the benefits of our bargain without your living up to your end of it."

John Paul did not answer, because there was no answer. That was exactly what John Paul was planning to do. Graff knew it, and John Paul didn't bother to deny it. Because knowing John Paul planned to cheat him did not change anything.

"I don't think he'll do that," said the woman.

But John Paul knew she was lying. She was quite concerned that he might do that. But she was even more concerned that Graff would walk away from the bargain John Paul was asking for. This was the confirmation John Paul needed. It really was very important to these people to get John Paul into Battle School. Therefore they would agree to a very bad bargain as long as it gave them some hope that he might go.

Or else they knew that no matter what they agreed to now, they could go back on their word whenever they wanted. After all, they were the International

Fleet, and the Wieczoreks were just a noncompliant family in a noncompliant country.

"What you don't know about me," said Graff, "is that I think very far ahead."

That reminded John Paul of what Andrew had said when he was teaching him to play chess. "You have to think ahead, the next move, the next move, the next move, to see where it's all going to lead." John Paul understood the principle as soon as Andrew explained it. But he stopped playing chess anyway, because he didn't care what happened to little plastic figures on a board of sixty-four squares.

Graff was playing chess, but not with little plastic figures. His game board was the world. And even though Graff was only a captain, he obviously came here with more authority – and more intelligence – than the colonel who had come before. When Graff said, "I think very far ahead," he was saying – this had to be his meaning – that he was willing to sacrifice a piece now and then in order to win the game, just like chess.

Maybe that meant he was willing to lie to John Paul now, and cheat him later. But no, there would be no reason to say anything at all. The only reason to say that was because Graff did *not* intend to cheat him. Graff was willing to be cheated, to knowingly enter into a bargain where the other person could win, and win completely – as long as he could see a way, farther down the road, for even such a defeat to turn to his advantage.

"You have to make us a promise that you'll never break," said John Paul. "Even if I don't go into space after all."

"I have the authority to make that promise," said Graff.

The woman clearly did not think so, though she said nothing.

"Is America a good place?" asked John Paul.

"There are an awful lot of Poles living there who think so," said Graff. "But it's not Poland."

"I want to see the whole world before I die," said John Paul. He had never told this to anyone before.

"Before you die," murmured Mother. "Why are you thinking about dying?"

As usual, she simply didn't understand. He wasn't thinking about dying. He was thinking about learning everything, and it was a simple fact that he had only a limited time in which to do it. Why did people get so upset when somebody mentioned dying? Did they think that if they didn't mention it, it would skip a few people and leave them alive forever? And how much faith in Christ did Mother really have, if she feared death so much she couldn't bear even to mention it, or hear her six-year-old child speak of it?

"Going to America is a start," said Graff. "And

American passports aren't restricted the way Polish passports are."

"We'll talk about it," said John Paul. "Come back later."

"Are you insane?" asked Helena as soon as they were out of earshot. "Isn't it obvious what the boy is planning?"

"No to the insanity, yes to the obviousness."

"These vids are going to be even more embarrassing for you than the earlier ones were for Sillain."

"Not really," said Graff.

"Why, because you intend to cheat the boy after all?"

"If I did that, then I truly would be insane." He stopped on the curb, apparently meaning to finish this conversation before getting back into the van with the others. Had he forgotten that what he was saying now was still being recorded?

No, he knew it. He wasn't speaking to her alone.

"Captain Rudolf," he said, "you saw, and everyone will see, that there was no way we could get that boy willingly into space. He doesn't want to go. He doesn't care about the war. That's what we've accomplished with this stupid repressive policy in the noncompliant nations. We have the best we've ever seen, and we can't use him because we've spent years creating a culture that hates the Hegemony and therefore the Fleet. We pissed on millions and millions of people in the name of some stupid population control laws, in defiance of their core beliefs and their community identity, and because the universe is statistically more likely to be ironic than not, of course our best chance at another commander like Mazer Rackham popped up among the ones we pissed on. I didn't do that, and only fools would blame me for it."

"So what was that all about? This agreement you promised? What's the *point*?"

"To get John Paul Wieczorek out of Poland, of course."

"But what difference does that make, if he won't go up to Battle School?"

"He's still . . . he still has a mind that processes human behavior the way some autistic savants process numbers or words. Don't you think it's a good thing to get him to a place where he can get a real education? And out of a place where he'll be constantly indoctrinated with hatred for the Hegemony and the I.F.?"

"I think that's beyond the scope of your authority," said Helena. "We're with the Battle School, not some Committee to Shape a Better Future by Moving Children Around."

"I'm thinking of Battle School," said Graff.

"To which John Paul Wieczorek will never go, as you just admitted."

"You're forgetting the research we've been con-
ducting. It may not be final in some technical
scientific sense, but it's already conclusive. People
reach their peak ability as military commanders
much earlier than we thought. Most of them in their
late teens. The same age when poets do their most
passionate and revolutionary work. And mathemati-
cians. They peak, and then it falls off. They coast on
what they learned back when they were still young
enough to learn. We know within a window of about
five years when we have to have our commander.
John Paul Wieczorek will already be too old when
that window opens. Past his peak."

"Obviously you've been given information I don't
have," said Helena.

"Or figured it out," said Graff. "Once it was obvious John Paul was never going to Battle School, my
mission changed. Now all that matters is we get John
Paul out of Poland and into a compliant country, and
we keep our word to him, absolutely, to the letter, so
he knows our promises will be kept even when we
know we've been cheated."

"What's the point of that?" asked Helena.

"Captain Rudolf, you're speaking without thinking."

He was right. So she thought.

"If we have more time before we need our commander," she said, "then do we have time for him to

marry and have children and then the children grow up enough to be the right age?"

"Just barely, yes. We have just barely enough time. If he marries young. If he marries somebody who is very, very brilliant so the gene mix is good."

"But you aren't going to try to control *that*, are you?"

"There are many steps on the continuum between controlling something and doing nothing at all."

"You really *do* think in the long term, don't you?"

"Think of me as Rumpelstiltskin."

She laughed. "All right, now I get it. You're giving him the wish of his heart, today. And then, long after he's forgotten, you're going to pop up and ask for his firstborn child."

Graff clapped an arm across her shoulder and walked with her toward the waiting van. "Only I don't have some stupid loophole that will let him get out of it if he can guess my name."

TEACHER'S PEST

THIS WAS NOT THE SECTION OF HUMAN COMMUNITY THAT John Paul Wiggin had tried to register for. It wasn't even his third choice. The university computer had assigned it to him because of some algorithm involving his seniority, how many first-choice classes he had received during his time there, and a slew of other considerations that meant nothing to him except that instead of getting one of the top-notch faculty he had come to this school to study with, he was going to have to suffer through the fumbling of a graduate student who knew little about the subject and less about how to teach it.

Maybe the algorithm's main criterion was how much he needed the course in order to graduate. They put him here because they knew he couldn't drop.

So he sat there in his usual front-row seat, looking at the backside of a teacher who looked like she was fifteen and dressed like she had been allowed to play in her mother's closet. She seemed to have a nice body and was probably trying to hide it behind frumpiness – but the fact that she *knew* she had something worth hiding suggested that she was no scientist. Probably not even a scholar.

I don't have time to help you work through your self-visualization problems, he said silently to the girl at the chalkboard. Nor to help you get past whatever weird method of teaching you're going to try out on us. What will it be? Socratic questioning? Devil's advocate? Therapy-group "discussion"? Belligerent toughness?

Give me a bored, worn-out wreck of a professor on the verge of retirement over a grad student every time.

Oh well. It was only this semester, next semester, a senior thesis, and then on to a fascinating career in government. Preferably in a position where he could work for the downfall of the Hegemony and the restoration of sovereignty for all nations.

Poland in particular, but he never said that to anyone, never even admitted that he had spent the first six years of his life in Poland. His documents all showed him and his whole family to be natural-born Americans. His parents' unlosable Polish accents proved that to be a lie, but considering that it was the Hegemony that had moved them to America and given them their false papers, it wasn't likely anybody was going to press the issue.

So write your diagrams on the board, Little Miss I-Want-to-Grow-Up-to-Be-a-Perfesser. I'll ace your tests and get my A and you'll never have a clue that the most arrogant, ambitious, and intelligent student on this campus was in your class.

At least that's what they told him he was, back when they were recruiting him. All except the arrogant part. They didn't actually *say* that. He just read it in their eyes.

"I wrote all this on the board," said the grad student with chalk, "because I want you to memorize it and, with any luck, understand it, because it's the basis of everything else we'll discuss in this class."

John Paul had already memorized it, of course, just by reading it. Because it was stuff he hadn't seen before in his outside reading, it was obvious her "method" was to try to be "cutting edge," full of the latest – and most likely to be wrong – research.

She looked right at him. "You seem particularly bored and contemptuous, Mr . . . Wiggin, is it? Is that because you already know about the community selection model of evolution?"

Oh, great. She was one of those "teachers" who had to have a goat in the class – someone to torment in order to score points.

"No, ma'am," said John Paul. "I came here hoping that you'd teach me everything about it." He kept every trace of sarcasm out of his tone; but of course that made it even more barbed and condescending.

He expected her to show annoyance at him, but

instead she merely turned to another student and began a dialogue. So either John Paul had scared her off, or she had been oblivious to his sarcasm and therefore had no idea she had been challenged.

The class wouldn't even be interesting as a blood sport. Too bad.

"'Human evolution is driven by community needs,'" she read from the board. "How is that possible, since genetic information is passed only by and to individuals?"

She was answered by the normal undergraduate silence. Fear of appearing stupid? Fear of seeming to care? Fear of seeming to be a suck-up? Of course, a few of the silent students were honestly stupid or apathetic, but most of them lived fear-driven lives.

Finally a tentative hand went up.

"Do communities, um, influence sexual selection? Like slanting eyes?"

"They do," said Miss Grad Student, "and the prevalence of the epicanthic fold in East Asia is a good example of that. But ultimately that's triv-ial – there is no actual survival value in it. I'm talking about good old rock-solid survival of the fittest. How can that be controlled by the commu-nity?"

"Killing people who don't fit in?" suggested another student.

John Paul slid down in his seat and stared at the ceiling. This far into their education, and they still had no understanding of basic principles.

"Mr. Wiggin seems to be bored with our discussion," said Miss Grad Student.

John Paul opened his eyes and scanned the board again. Ah, she *had* written her name there. Theresa Brown. "Yes, Ms. Brown, I am," he said.

"Is this because you know the answer, or because you don't care?"

"I don't know the answer," said John Paul, "but neither does anyone else in the room except you, so until you decide to tell us instead of engaging in this enchanting voyage of discovery in which you let the passengers steer the ship, it's naptime."

There were a few gasps and a couple of chuckles.

"So you have no ideas about how the statement on the board might be either true or false?"

"I suppose," said John Paul, "that the theory you're suggesting is that because living in communities makes humans far more likely to survive, and to have opportunities to mate, and to bring their children to adulthood, then whatever individual human traits strengthen the community will, in the long run, be the ones most likely to get passed along to each new generation."

She blinked. "Yes," she said. "That's right." And then she blinked again. Apparently he had interrupted her lesson plan by getting to the answer immediately.

"But what I wonder," said John Paul, "is this: Since human communities depend on adaptability in order to thrive, then it isn't just one set of traits that strengthen the community. So community life should promote variety, not a narrow range of traits."

"That would be true," said Ms. Brown, "and indeed *is* true in the main, except that there are only a few types of human communities that actually survive long enough to improve the chances of individual survival."

She walked to the board and wiped out a swath of material that John Paul had just blown through by cutting to the chase. In its place, she wrote two headings: TRIBAL and CIVIL.

"There are two models that all successful human communities follow," she said. Then she turned to John Paul. "How would you define a 'successful' community, Mr. Wiggin?"

"One that maximized the ability of its members to survive and reproduce," he said.

"Oh, if only that were true," she said. "But it's *not* true. Most human communities demand anti-survival behavior from large numbers of their members. The obvious example would be war, in which members of a community risk their own death – usually at the very age when they are about to begin family life. Many of them die. How can you possibly pass on the willingness to die before reproduction? Those who have this trait are the least likely to reproduce."

"But only males," said John Paul.

"There are women in the military, Mr. Wiggin."

"In very small numbers," said John Paul, "because the traits that make good soldiers are far less common in women, and the willingness to go to war is rare in women."

"Women fight savagely and die willingly to protect their children," said Ms. Brown.

"Exactly – *their* children. *Not* the community as a whole," said John Paul. He was making this up as he went along, but it made sense and was interesting – so he was quite willing to let her play the Socratic questioning game.

"And yet women are the ones who form the tightest community bonds," she said.

"And the most rigid hierarchies," said John Paul. "But they do it by social sanctions, not by violence."

"So you're saying that violence in males but civility in women is promoted by community life."

"Not violence," said John Paul. "But the willingness to sacrifice for a cause."

"In other words," said Ms. Brown, "men believe the stories their communities tell them. Enough to die and kill. And women don't?"

"They believe them enough to . . ." John Paul

paused a moment, thinking back on what he knew about learned and unlearned sex differences. "Women have to be willing to raise their sons in a community that might require them to die. So men and women all have to believe the story."

"And the story they believe," said Ms. Brown, "is that males are expendable and females are not."

"To a degree, anyway."

"And why would this be a useful story for a community to believe?" She directed this question to the class at large.

And the answers came quickly enough, because some of the students, at least, were following the conversation. "Because even if half the men die, all the women will still be able to reproduce." "Because it provides an outlet for male aggressiveness." "Because you have to be able to defend the community's resources."

John Paul watched as Theresa Brown fielded each response and riffed on it.

"*Do* communities that suffered terrible losses in war in fact abandon monogamy or do a large number of women live their lives without reproducing?" She had the example of France, Germany, and Britain after the bloodletting of World War I.

"Does war come about *because* of male aggressiveness? Or is male aggressiveness a trait that communities have to promote in order to win wars?

Is it the community that drives the trait, or the trait that drives the community?" Which John Paul realized was the very crux of the theory she was putting forth – and he rather liked the question.

"And what," she finally asked, "are the resources a community has to protect?"

Food, they said. Water. Shelter. But these obvious answers did not seem to be what she was looking for. "All these are important, but you're missing the most important one."

To his own surprise, John Paul found himself wanting to come up with the right answer. He had never expected to feel that way in a class taught by a grad student.

What community resource could be more important to the survival of the community than food, water, or shelter?

He raised his hand.

"Mr. Wiggin seems to think he knows." She looked at him.

"Wombs," he said.

"As a community resource," she said.

"As the community," said John Paul. "Women *are* community."

She smiled. "*That* is the great secret."

There were howls of protest from other students. About how men have always run most communities. How women were treated like property.

"*Some* men," she answered. "*Most* men are treated far more like property than women. Because women are almost never simply thrown away, while men are thrown away by the thousands in time of war."

"But men still *rule*," a student protested.

"Yes, they do," said Ms. Brown. "The handful of alpha males rule, while all the other males become tools. But even the ruling males know that the most vital resource of the community is the women, and any community that is going to survive has to bend all its efforts to one primary task – to promote the ability of women to reproduce and bring their offspring to adulthood."

"So what about societies that selectively abort or kill off their girl children?" insisted a student.

"Those would be societies that had decided to die, wouldn't they?" said Ms. Brown.

Consternation. Uproar.

It was an interesting model. Communities that killed off their girls would have fewer girls reach reproductive age. Therefore they would be less successful in maintaining a high population. He raised his hand.

"Enlighten us, Mr. Wiggin," she said.

"I just have a question," he said. "Couldn't there be an advantage in having an excess of males?"

"It must not be an important one," said Ms. Brown, "because the vast majority of human communities – especially the ones that survive longest – have shown a willingness to throw away males, not females. Besides, killing female babies gives you a higher *proportion* of males, but a lower absolute *number* of males, because there are fewer females to give birth to them."

"But what about when resources are scarce?" a student asked.

"What about it?" said Ms. Brown.

"I mean, don't you have to reduce the population to sustainable levels?"

Suddenly the room was very quiet.

Ms. Brown laughed. "Anyone want to try an answer to that?"

No one spoke.

"And why have we suddenly become silent?" she asked.

She waited.

Finally someone murmured, "The population laws."

"Ah," she said. "Politics. We have a worldwide decision to decrease the human population by limiting the number of births to two per couple. And you don't want to talk about it."

The silence said that they didn't even want to talk about the fact that they didn't want to talk about it.

"The human race is fighting for its survival against

an alien invasion," she said, "and in the process, we have decided to *limit* our reproduction."

"Somebody named Brown," said John Paul, "ought to know how dangerous it can be to go on record as opposing the population laws."

She looked at him icily. "This is a science class, not a political debate," she said. "There are community traits that promote survival of the individual, and individual traits that promote the survival of the community. In this class, we are not afraid to go where the evidence takes us."

"What if it takes us out of any chance of getting a job?" asked a student.

"I'm here to teach the students who want to learn what I know," she said. "If you're one of that happy number, then aren't we both lucky. If you're not, I don't much care. But I'm not going to *not* teach you something because knowing it might somehow make you less employable."

"So is it true," asked a girl in the front row, "that he really *is* your father?"

"Who?" asked Ms. Brown.

"You know," the girl said. "Hinckley Brown."

Hinckley Brown. The military strategist whose book was still the bible of the International Fleet – but who resigned from the I.F. and went into seclusion because he refused to go along with the population laws.

"And this would be relevant to you because . . .?" asked Ms. Brown.

The answer was belligerent. "Because we have a right to know if you're teaching us science or your religion."

That's right, thought John Paul. Hinckley Brown was a Mormon, and they were noncompliant.

Noncompliant like John Paul's own parents, who were Polish Catholics.

Noncompliant like John Paul intended to be, as soon as he found somebody he wanted to marry. Somebody who also wanted to stick it to the Hegemony and their two-children-per-family law.

"What if," said Ms. Brown, "the findings of science happen to coincide, on a particular point, with the beliefs of a religion? Do we reject the science in order to reject the religion?"

"What if the science gets influenced by the religion?" demanded the student.

"Fortunately," said Ms. Brown, "the question is not only stupid and offensive, it's also moot. Because whatever blood relationship I might or might not have with the famous Admiral Brown, the only thing that matters is my science and, if you happen to be suspicious, my religion."

"So what is your religion?" the student said.

"My religion," said Ms. Brown, "is to try to falsify all hypotheses. Including your hypothesis that teachers should be judged according to their parentage or their membership in a group. If you find me teaching something that cannot be adduced from the evidence, then you can make your complaint. And since it seems particularly important to you to avoid any possibility of an idea contaminated by Hinckley Brown's beliefs, I will drop you from the class . . . right . . . now."

By the end of the sentence she was jabbing instructions at her desk, which was sitting atop the podium. She looked up. "There. You can leave now and go to the department offices to arrange to be admitted to a different section of this class."

The student was flabbergasted. "I don't want to drop this class."

"I don't recall asking you what you wanted," said Ms. Brown. "You're a bigot and a troublemaker, and I don't have to keep you in my class. That goes for the rest of you. We will follow the evidence, we will challenge ideas, but we will not challenge the personal life of the teacher. Anyone else want to drop?"

In that moment, John Paul Wiggin fell in love.

Theresa let the exhilaration of Human Community carry her for several hours. The class hadn't started well – the Wiggin boy looked to be a troublemaker. But it turned out he was as smart as he was arrogant, and it sparked the brightest kids in the class, and all in all it was exactly the kind of thing Theresa had always loved about teaching: a group of people thinking the same thoughts, conceiving the same universe, becoming, for just a few moments, one.

The Wiggin "boy." She had to laugh at her own attitude. She was probably younger than he was. But she felt so old. She'd been in grad school for several years now, and it felt as if the weight of the world were on her shoulders. It wasn't enough to have her own career to worry about, there was the constant pressure of her father's crusade. Everything she did was interpreted by everyone as if her father were speaking through her, as if he somehow controlled her mind and heart.

Why shouldn't they think so? He did.

But she refused to think about him. She was a scientist, even if she was a bit on the theoretical side. She was not a child anymore. More to the point, she was not a soldier in his army, a fact that he had never recognized and never would – especially now that his "army" was so small and weak.

Then she got beeped for a meeting with the dean.

Grad students didn't get called in for meetings with the dean. And the fact that the secretary claimed to have no idea what the meeting was about or who else would be there filled her with foreboding.

The late summer weather was quite warm, even this far north, but since Theresa lived an indoor life she rarely noticed it. Certainly she hadn't dressed for the afternoon temperature. She was dripping with sweat by the time she got to the graduate school offices, and instead of having a few minutes in the air-conditioning to cool down, the secretary rushed her right into the dean's office.

Worse and worse.

There was the dean and her entire dissertation committee. And Dr. Howell, who had apparently returned from retirement just for this occasion. Whatever this occasion was.

They barely took time for the basic courtesies before they broke the news to her. "The foundation has decided to withdraw funding unless we remove you from the project."

"On what grounds?" she asked.

"Your age, mostly," said the dean. "You *are* extraordinarily young to be running a research project of this scope."

"But it's my project. It only exists because I thought of it."

"I know it seems unfair," said the dean. "But we won't let this interfere with your progress toward your doctorate."

"Won't let it interfere?" She laughed in consternation. "It took a year to get this grant, even though it's one with obvious value for the current world situation. Even if I had a new research project on the back burner, you can't pretend that this won't postpone my degree by years."

"We recognize the problem this is causing you, but we're prepared to grant you your degree with a project of . . . less . . . scope."

"Help me understand this," she said. "You trust me so much that you'd grant me a degree without caring about my dissertation. Yet you don't trust me enough to let me even take part in a vital project that I designed. Who's going to run it?"

She looked at her committee chairman. He blushed.

"This isn't even your area," she said to him. "It's nobody's area but mine."

"As you said," her chairman answered, "you designed the project. We'll follow your plan exactly. Whatever data emerges, it will have the same value regardless of who heads it up."

She stood up. "Of course I'm leaving," she said. "You can't do this to me."

"Theresa," said Dr. Howell.

"Oh," said Theresa, "is it your job to get me to go along with this?"

"Theresa," repeated the old woman. "You know perfectly well what this is about."

"No, I don't," said Theresa.

"Nobody here at this table will admit it, but . . . it's only 'mostly' about how young you are."

"So what's the 'partly' that's left over?" asked Theresa.

"I think," said Dr. Howell, "that if your father came out of retirement, suddenly there'd be no objection to one so young running an important research project."

Theresa looked around at the others. "You can't be serious."

"Nobody has come out and said it," said the dean, "but they *have* pointed out that the impetus for this came from the foundation's main customer."

"The Hegemony," said her chairman.

"So I'm a hostage to my father's politics."

"Or his religion," said the dean. "Or whatever it is that's driving him."

"And you'll let your academic program be manipulated for . . . for . . ."

"The university depends on grants," said the dean. "Imagine what will happen to us if, one by one, our grant applications start being refused. The Hegemony has enormous influence. Everywhere."

"In other words," said Dr. Howell, "there really isn't anywhere else you can go. We're one of the *most* independent universities, and we aren't free. That's why they're determined to grant you a doctorate despite the fact that you can't do your research. Because you deserve one, and they know this is grossly unfair."

"So what's to stop them from keeping me from teaching, too? Who would even *have* me? A Ph.D. who can't show her research – what a joke I'd be."

"We'd hire you," said the dean.

"Why?" demanded Theresa. "A charity case? What could I possibly accomplish at a university where I can't do research?"

Dr. Howell sighed. "Because of course you'd continue to run the project. Who else could manage it?"

"Without my name on it," said Theresa.

"It's important research," said Dr. Howell. "The survival of the human race is at stake. There's a war on, you know."

"Then tell that to the foundation and get them to tell the Hegemony to –"

"Theresa," said Dr. Howell. "Your name won't be on the project. It won't be listed as your dissertation. But everybody in the field will know *exactly* who did it. You'll have a tenure track position here, a doctorate, and a dissertation whose authorship is an open secret. All we're really asking you to do is swallow hard and get along with the ridiculous requirements that have been forced on us – and no, we will *not* listen to your decision now. In fact, we will ignore anything you say or do for the next three days. Talk to your father. Talk to any of us, all you want. But no answer until you've had a chance to get over the shock."

"Don't treat me like a child."

"No, my dear," said Dr. Howell. "Our plan is to treat you like a human being that we value too much to . . . what is your favorite term? . . . 'throw away.'"

The dean stood up. "And with that, we will adjourn this terrible meeting, in the hope that you will stay with us under these cruel circumstances." And he walked out of the room.

The members of her committee shook her hand – she accepted their handshakes numbly – and Dr. Howell hugged her and whispered, "Your father's war will have many casualties before it's through. You may bleed for him, but for God's sake, please don't *die* for him. Professionally speaking."

The meeting – and, quite possibly, her career – was over.

John Paul spotted her crossing the quad and made it a point to be leaning against the stair rail at the entrance to the Human Sciences building.

"Isn't it a little hot for a sweater?" he asked.

She paused, looking at him just long enough that he figured she must be trying to remember who he was.

"Wiggin," she said.

"John Paul," he added, holding out his hand.

She looked at it, then at his face. "Isn't it a little hot for a sweater," she said vaguely.

"Funny, I was just thinking that," said John Paul. Clearly this girl was distracted by something.

"Is this some technique that works for you? Telling a girl she is dressed inappropriately? Or is it merely the mention of clothing that ought to come off?"

"Wow," said John Paul. "You saw right to my soul. And yes, it works on most women. I have to beat them back with a stick."

Again a momentary pause. Only this time he didn't wait for her to come up with some put-down. If he was going to recover any chance, it would take some fast misdirection.

"I'm sorry that I spoke the thought that came into my head," said John Paul. "I said 'Isn't it a little hot for a sweater?' because it's a little hot for a sweater. And because I wanted to see if you had a minute I could talk to you."

"I don't," said Ms. Brown. She walked past him toward the door of the building.

He followed. "Actually, we're in the middle of your office hours right now, aren't we?"

"So go to my office," she said.

"Mind if I walk with you?"

She stopped. "It's not my office hours," she said.

"I knew I should have checked," he said.

She pushed open the door and entered the building.

He followed. "Look at it this way – there won't be a line outside your door."

"I teach a low-prestige, bad-time-of-day section of Human Community," said Ms. Brown. "There's never a line outside my door."

"Long enough I ended up clear out there," said John Paul.

They were at the foot of the stairs leading up to the second floor. She faced him again. "Mr. Wiggin, you are better than average when it comes to cleverness, and perhaps another day I might have enjoyed our badinage."

He grinned. A woman who would say "badinage" to a man was rare – a tiny subset of the women who actually knew the word.

"Yes, yes," she said, as if trying to answer his smile. "Today isn't a good day. I won't see you in my office. I have things on my mind."

"I have nothing on mine," said John Paul, "and I'm a good listener, amazingly discreet."

She walked on up the stairs ahead of him. "I find that hard to believe."

"Oh, you can believe it," he said. "Practically everything in my school records, for instance, is a lie, and yet I never tell anybody."

Again it took her a moment to get the joke, but this time she answered with one yip of laughter. Progress.

"Ms. Brown," he said, "I really did want to talk to you about ideas from class. Whatever you might have thought, I wasn't coming on to you with some line, and I'm not trying to be clever with you. I was just surprised that you seem to be teaching a version of Human Community that isn't like the standard stuff – I mean, there's nothing about it in the textbook, which is all about primates and bonding and hierarchies –"

"We'll be covering all that."

"It's been a long time since I've had a professor who knew things I hadn't already learned through my own reading."

"I don't know things," she said. "I'm trying to find out things. There's a difference."

"Ms. Brown," said John Paul, "I'm not going to go away."

She stopped at the door of her office. "And why is that? Apart from the fact that I *could* take that as a threat to stalk me."

"Ms. Brown," said John Paul. "I think you might be smarter than me."

She laughed in his face. "Of course I'm smarter than you."

He pointed at her triumphantly. "See? And you're arrogant about it, too. We have so much in common. Are you really going to shut this door in my face?"

She shut the door in his face.

*

Theresa tried to work on her next lecture. She tried to read several scientific journals. She couldn't concentrate. All she could think about was them taking her project away from her – not the work, just the credit. She tried to convince herself that what mattered was the science, not the prestige. She was *not* one of those pathetic on-the-make grad students who were all about career, with research serving as no more than a stepping stone. It was the research itself that she cared about. So why not recognize the political realities, accept their quislingesque "offer," and be content?

It's not about the credit. It's about the Hegemony perverting the whole system of science as a means of extortion. Not that science is particularly pure, except compared to politics.

She found herself displaying the data of her students on her desk, calling up their pictures and records and glancing at them. In the back of her mind she knew she was looking for John Paul Wiggin. What he had said about his school records being a lie intrigued her. And looking him up was such a trivial task that she could do it even while fretting over what they were doing to her.

John Paul Wiggin. Second child of Brian and Anne Wiggin; older brother named Andrew. Born in Racine, Wisconsin, so apparently he was an expert on what weather was appropriate for sweaters. Straight

A's in the Racine public school system. Graduated a year early, valedictorian, lots of clubs, three years of soccer. Exactly what the admissions people were looking for. And his record here was just as good – nothing less than an *A*, and not an easy course on the list. A year younger than her. And yet . . . no declared major, which suggested that even though he had enough credit hours that he could graduate at the end of this year, he still hadn't settled on a field of study.

A bright dilettante. A time-waster.

Except that he said it was all a lie.

Which parts? Surely not the grades – he was clearly bright enough to earn them. And what else could possibly be a lie? What would be the point?

He was just a boy trying to be intriguing. He spotted that she was young for a teacher, and in his school-centered life, the teacher was at the pinnacle of prestige. Maybe he tried to ingratiate himself with all his teachers. If he became a problem, she'd have to ask around and see if it was a pattern.

The desk beeped to tell her she had a call.

She pressed NO PICTURE and then ANSWER. She knew who it was, of course, even though no identity or telephone number appeared.

"Hello, Father," she said.

"Turn on the picture, darlin', I want to see your face."

"You'll have to search through your memory," she said. "Father, I don't want to talk right now."

"Those bastards can't do this to you."

"Yes they can."

"I'm sorry, darlin', I never meant my own decisions to impinge on you."

"If the Buggers blow up planet Earth," she said, "because you aren't there to stop them, that will impinge on me."

"And if we defeat the Buggers but we've lost everything that makes it worth being human —"

"Father, don't give me the stump speech, I've got it down pat."

"Darlin', I'm just saying that I wouldn't have done this if I'd known they'd try to take away your career."

"Oh, right, you'll put the whole human race at risk, but not your daughter's career."

"I'm not putting anything at risk. They already have everything I know. I'm a theorist, not a commander — it's a commander they need now, a whole different skill set. So this is really just . . . what, their fit of pique because my leaving the I.F. was bad public relations for them and —"

"Father, didn't you notice that I didn't call you?"

"You only just found out."

"Yes, and who told you? Someone from the school?"

"No, it was Grasdolf, he has a friend at the foundation and —"

"Exactly."

Father sighed. "You're such a cynic."

"What good does it do to take a hostage if you don't send a ransom note?"

"Grasdolf is a friend, they're just using him, and I meant what I said about —"

"Father, you might think, for a moment, that you'd give up your quixotic crusade in order to make my life easier, but the fact is you won't, and you know it and I know it. I don't even *want* you to give it up. I don't even care. All right? So your conscience is clear, their attempt at extortion was bound to fail, the school is taking care of me after their fashion, and hey, I've got a smart, cute, and annoyingly conceited boy in one of my classes trying to hit on me, so life is just about perfect."

"Aren't you just the noblest martyr."

"See how quickly it turns into a fight?"

"Because you won't talk to me, you just say whatever you think will make me go away."

"Apparently I still haven't found it. But am I getting warm?"

"Why do you do this? Why do you close the door on everybody who cares about you?"

"As far as I know, I've only closed the door on people who want something from me."

"And what do you think I want?"

"To be known as the most brilliant military

theorist of all time *and* still have your family as devoted to you as we might have been if we had actually known you. And *see?* I don't want this conversation, we've been through it all before, and when I hang up on you, which I'm about to do, please don't keep calling me back and leaving pathetic messages on my desk. And yes, I love you and I'm really fine about this so it's over, period, good-bye."

She hung up.

Only then was she able to cry.

Tears of frustration, that's all they were. Nothing. She needed the release. It wouldn't even matter if other people knew she was crying – as long as her research was dispassionate, she didn't have to *live* that way.

When she stopped crying she laid her head down on her arms on the desk and maybe she even dozed for a while. Must have done. It was late afternoon. She was hungry and she needed to pee. She hadn't eaten since breakfast and she always got lightheaded about four if she skipped lunch.

The student records were still on her desk. She wiped them and got up and straightened her sweaty clothing and thought, It really is too warm for a sweater, especially a sloppy thick bulky one like this. But she didn't have a shirt on underneath so there was no solution for it, she'd just have to go home as a ball of sweat.

If she ever went home during daylight hours she

might have learned to dress in a way that would be adaptable to afternoon temperatures. But right now she had no interest at all in working late. Somebody else's name would be on anything she did, right? Screw them all and the grants they rode in on.

She opened the door . . .

And there was the Wiggin boy, sitting with his back to the door, laying out plastic silverware on paper napkins. The smell of hot food nearly made her step back into the office.

He looked up at her but did not smile. "Spring rolls from Hunan," he said, "chicken satay from My Thai, salads from Garden Green, and if you want to wait a few more minutes, we've got stuffed mushrooms from Trompe L'Oeuf."

"All I want," she said, "is to pee. I don't want to do it on insane students camped at my door, so if you'd move to one side . . ."

He moved.

When she had washed up she thought of not going back to her office. The office door had locked behind her. She had her purse. She owed nothing to this boy.

But curiosity got the better of her. She wasn't going to eat any of the food, but she had to find out the answer to one question.

"How did you know when I was coming out?" she demanded, as she stood over the picnic he had prepared.

"I didn't," he said. "The pizza and the burritos hit the garbage half an hour ago and fifteen minutes ago, respectively."

"You mean you've been ordering food at intervals so that —"

"So that whenever you came out, there'd be something hot and/or fresh."

"And/or?"

He shrugged. "If you don't like it, that's fine. Of course, I'm on a budget because what I live on is whatever they pay me for custodial work in the physical sciences building, so this is half my week's wages down the toilet if you don't like it."

"You really are a liar," she said. "I know what they pay part-time custodians and it would take you two weeks to pay for all this."

"So I guess pity won't get you to sit down and eat with me."

"Yes it will," she said. "But not pity for you."

"For whom, then?" he asked.

"For myself, of course," she said, sitting down. "I wouldn't touch the mushrooms — I'm allergic to shi-itake and Oeuf seems to think they're the only true mushroom. And the satay is bound to be cold because they never serve it hot even in the restaurant."

He wafted a paper napkin over her crossed legs and handed her a knife and fork. "So do you want to know which part of my records are a lie?" he asked.

"I don't care," she said, "and I didn't look up your records."

He pointed to his own desk. "I long since installed my own monitoring software in the database. I know whenever my stuff gets accessed, and by whom."

"That's absurd," she said. "They sweep for viruses on the school system twice a day."

"They sweep for known viruses and detectable anomalies," he said.

"But you tell your secret to *me*?"

"Only because you lied to me," said the Wiggin boy. "Habitual liars don't rat each other out."

"All right," she said. Meaning, all right, what's the lie? But then she tasted her spring roll and said, "All right," again, this time meaning, Good food, just right.

"Glad you liked them. I have them cut down on the ginger, which allows the taste of the vegetables to come through. Though of course I dip them in this incredibly robust soy-and-chili-and-mustard sauce, so I have no idea what they actually taste like."

"Let me try the sauce," she said. He was right, it was so good she contemplated pouring some on her salad as dressing. Or just drinking it from the little plastic cup.

"And in case you wanted to know what part of my records is a lie, I can give you the whole list: Everything. The only true statement in my records is 'the.'"

"That's absurd. Who would do that? What's the point? Are you some protected witness to a hideous crime?"

"I wasn't born in Wisconsin, I was born in Poland. I lived there till I was six. I was only in Racine for two weeks prior to coming here, so if I met anybody from there, I could talk about landmarks and convince them I'd really lived there."

"Poland," she said. And, because of her father's crusade against the population laws, she couldn't help but register the fact that it was a noncompliant country.

"Yep, we're illegal emigrants from Poland. Slipped past the web of Hegemony guards. Or maybe we should say, sublegal."

To people like that, Hinckley Brown was a hero. "Oh," she said, disappointed. "I see. This picnic isn't about me, it's about my father."

"Why, who's your father?" asked John Paul.

"Oh, come on, Wiggin, you heard the girl in class this morning. My father is Hinckley Brown."

John Paul shrugged as if he'd never heard of him.

"Come on," she said. "It was all over the vids last year. My father resigns from the I.F. because of the populations laws, and your family is from Poland. Coincidence? I don't think so."

He laughed. "You really are suspicious."

"I can't believe you didn't get Hunan wontons."

"Didn't know if you'd like them. They're an acquired taste. I wanted to play it safe."

"By spreading a picnic on the floor in front of my office door, and throwing away whatever food got cold before I came out? How safe can you get?"

"Let's see," said Wiggin. "Other lies. Oh, my name isn't Wiggin, it's Wieczorek. And I have way more than one sib."

"Valedictorian?" she said.

"I would have been, except I persuaded the administration to skip over me."

"Why is that?"

"Don't want any pictures. Don't want any resentment from other students."

"Ah, a recluse. Well, that explains everything."

"It doesn't explain why you were crying in your office," said the Wiggin boy.

She reached into her mouth and took out the last bite of spring roll, which she had only just put in. "Sorry I can't return any of the other used food," she said. "But you can't buy my personal life for the price of a few takeout items." She set the morsel of saliva-covered spring roll on her napkin.

"You think I didn't notice what they did to your project?" asked the Wiggin boy. "Firing you from it when it's your own idea. I'd've cried, too."

"I'm not fired," she said.

"Scuzi, bella dona, but the records don't lie."

"That's the most ridiculous . . ." Then she realized that he was grinning.

"Ha ha," she said.

"I don't want to buy your personal life," said the Wiggin boy. "I want to learn everything you know about Human Community."

"Then come to class. And next time bring the treats *there*, to share."

"The treats," said the Wiggin boy, "aren't for sharing. They're for you."

"Why? What do you want from me?"

"I want to be the one who, when I telephone you, I never make you cry."

"At the moment," she said, "you're only making me want to scream."

"That will pass," said the Wiggin boy. "Oh, and another lie is my age. I'm really two years older than the records say. They started me in American schools late, because I had to learn English and . . . there were certain complications about a contract that they asserted I had no intention of fulfilling. But after they gave up, they changed my age so nobody would see how chronologically misplaced I was."

"They?"

"The Hegemony," said the Wiggin boy.

Only he wasn't a mere boy, she supposed. A man. John Paul Wiggin. It was wrenching to start thinking of him with a name. Unprofessional. Perilous.

"You actually got the Hegemony to give up?"

"I don't know that they gave up completely. I think they merely changed goals."

"All right, now I'm actually curious."

"Instead of being irritated and hungry?"

"In addition to those."

"Curious about what?"

"What was your quarrel with the Hegemony?"

"The I.F., actually. They thought I ought to go to Battle School."

"They can't force you to do that."

"I know. But as a condition of going to Battle School I got them to move my whole family out of Poland first and set things up so that the sanctions against oversized families didn't apply to us."

"Those sanctions are enforced in America, too."

"Yes, if you make a big deal about it," said John Paul. "Like your father. Like your whole church."

"Not my church."

"Right, of course, you're the only person in history who is completely immune to her religious upbringing."

She wanted to argue with him, but she knew the science his assertion was based on that showed the impossibility of escaping from the core worldview instilled in children by their parents. Even though she had long since repudiated it, it was still inside her, so that there was a constant argument, her parents' voices sniping at her, her own inner voice arguing with them. "Even people who just quietly have lots of children get zapped by the law," she said.

"My older sibs were set up with relatives. Enough of us were boarded out that there were never more than two children home. We were called nieces and nephews when we 'visited.'"

"And they still maintained all this for you, even after you refused to go to Battle School?"

"Sort of," said John Paul. "They actually made me go to ground school for a while, but I went on strike. And then they talked about sending us all back to Poland or getting sanctions against us here in America."

"So why didn't they?"

"I had the deal in writing."

"Since when has that ever stopped a determined government?"

"Oh, it wasn't because the contract was particularly enforceable. It was the fact that it existed at all. I merely threatened to make it public. And they couldn't deny that they had fiddled with the population laws because here we were, physical evidence that they had made an exception."

"Government can make all kinds of inconvenient evidence disappear."

"I know," said John Paul. "Which is why I think they still have an agenda. They couldn't get me into

Battle School, but they let me stay here in America and my whole family, too. Like the devil in all the old sell-your-soul stories, they're going to collect sometime."

"And that doesn't bother you?"

"I'll deal with it when their plan emerges. So what about you? Their plan for you is already quite clear."

"Not really," she said. "On the surface, it looks like typical Hegemony behavior – punish the daughter to get the highly visible father to cease his rebellion against the population laws. Unfortunately, my father grew up on the movie 'A Man for All Seasons' and he thinks he's Thomas More. I think it only disappointed him that it was my head they cut off instead of his, professionally speaking."

"Only you think there's more to it than that?"

"The dean and my committee are still going to give me my degree and have me head the project – I'm just not going to get any credit for it. Well, that's annoying, yes, but in the long run it's trivial. Don't you think?"

"Maybe they think you're a careerist like they all are."

"But they know my father's not. They can't actually think this would make him give in. Or that it would even get me to try to pressure him."

"Don't underestimate the stupidity of the government."

"This is wartime," she said. "An emergency they

really believe in. The tolerance for idiots in powerful positions is very low right now. No, I don't think they're stupid. I think I don't understand their plan yet."

He nodded. "So we're both waiting to see what they have in mind."

"I suppose."

"And you're going to stay here and head your project."

"For now."

"Once you start, you won't let go until you have your results."

"Some of the results won't be in for twenty years."

"Longitudinal study?"

"Observational, really. And in a sense it's absurd — trying to mathematicize history. But I've set up the criteria for measuring the key components of long-lived civil societies, and the triggers that collapse a civil society back into tribalism. Is it possible for a civitas to last forever? Or is breakdown an inevitable product of a successful civil society? Or is there a hunger for the tribe that always works its way to the surface? Right now it doesn't look good for the human race. My preliminary assessment shows that when a civil society is mature and successful, the citizens become complacent and to satisfy various needs they reinvent tribes that eventually collapse the society from the inside."

"So both failure and success lead to failure."

"The only question is whether it's inevitable."

"Sounds like useful information."

"I can tell them right now that population controls are about as stupid a move as they could make."

"Depending on the goal," said John Paul.

She thought about that for a moment. "You mean they might not be trying to make the Hegemony last?"

"What *is* the Hegemony? Just a collection of nations that banded together to fight off one enemy. What if we win? Why would the Hegemony be permitted to continue? Why would nations like this one submit to authority?"

"They might, if the Hegemony were well-governed."

"That's the fear. If only a few nations want out, then the others might hold them all in, like the North did to the South in the American Civil War. So if you intend to break up the Hegemony, you make sure as many nations and tribes as possible detest it and regard it as an oppressor."

Well, aren't I the stupid one, thought Theresa. In all these years, neither Father nor I has ever questioned the motive of the population laws. "Do you really think there's anybody in the Hegemony who's subtle enough to think of something like that?"

"It doesn't take a lot. A few key players. Why do

they make such a divisive program the absolute linchpin of the war program? The population laws don't help the economy. We have plenty of raw materials, and we'd actually accomplish more, faster, if we had a steadily growing world population. On every count it's counterproductive. And yet it's the one dogma that nobody dares to question. Like the way the class reacted when you just touched on the subject this morning."

"So if the last thing they want is for the Hegemony to last, why would they allow my project to continue?"

"Maybe the people who push for the population laws aren't the same people as the ones who are letting your project go on under the table."

"And if my father were still in the game, he might even know who."

"Or not. He was with the I.F. These people might be nonmilitary. Might be within various national governments and not in the Hegemony at all. What if your project is being quietly supported by the American government while they make a show of enforcing the population laws for the Hegemony?"

"Either way, I'm just a tool."

"Come on, Theresa," he said. "We're all tools in somebody's kit. But that doesn't mean we can't make tools out of other people. Or figure out interesting things to use ourselves for."

When he called her by name, it annoyed her. Well, maybe not annoyed. She felt *something*, anyway, and it made her uncomfortable. "This was a very good picnic, Mr. Wiggin, but I'm afraid you think it's changed our relationship."

"Of course it has," said John Paul, "since we didn't have one and now we do."

"We had one – teacher and student."

"We still have that one – in class."

"That's the only one we have."

"Not really," said John Paul. "Because I'm also a teacher and you're a student, when it comes to the things I know and you don't."

"I'll let you know when that happens. I'll enroll in your class."

"We make each other think better," he said. "Together, we're smarter. And when you consider how incredibly bright we both are apart, it's downright scary to combine us."

"Intellectual nuclear fusion," she said, mocking the idea.

Only it wasn't mockery, was it? It was quite possibly true.

"Of course, our relationship is grossly unbalanced," said John Paul.

"In what way?" she asked, suspecting that he would find some clever way of saying that he was smarter or more creative.

"Because I'm in love with you," said John Paul, "and you still think I'm an annoying student."

She knew what she ought to feel. She ought to find his attentions touching and sweet. She also knew what she ought to do. She should immediately tell him that while she was flattered by his feelings, they would never lead to anything because she didn't have those feelings toward him and never would.

Only she didn't know that. Not for sure. There was something breathtaking about his declaring himself like this.

"We only met today," she said.

"And what I feel is only the first stirring of love," he said. "If you treat me like a hairball, then of course I'll get over it. But I don't want to get over it. I want to keep getting to know you better and better, so I can love you more and more. I think you're a match for me, and more than a match. Where else am I ever going to find a woman who just might be smarter than I am?"

"Since when is that what a man is looking for?"

"Only stupid men trying *to seem* smart need to be with dumb women. Only weak men trying to look strong are attracted to compliant women. Surely there's something about that in Human Community."

"So you saw me this morning and —"

"I *heard* you this morning, I *talked* with you, you made me think, I made *you* think, and it was electric.

It was just as electric a moment ago as we sat here trying to outguess the Hegemony. I think they ought to be scared to death, having the two of us sitting here together plotting against them."

"Is that what we were doing?"

"We both hate them," said John Paul.

"I don't know that I do," said Theresa. "My father does. But I'm not my father."

"You hate the Hegemony because it isn't what it pretends to be," said John Paul. "If it were really a government of the whole human race, with a commitment to democracy and fairness and growth and freedom, then neither of us would oppose it. Instead it's merely a temporary alliance which leaves a lot of evil governments intact underneath its umbrella. And now that we know that those governments are manipulating things to try to make sure the Hegemony *never* becomes the thing we want it to be, then what are two brilliant kids like us to do, except plot to overthrow the present Hegemony and put something better in its place?"

"I'm not interested in politics."

"You live and breathe politics," said John Paul. "You just call it 'community studies' and pretend you're only interested in observing and understanding. But someday you'll have children and they'll live in this world and you already care very much what kind of world they live in."

She didn't like this at all. "What makes you think I intend ever to have children?"

He just chuckled.

"I'm certainly not going to have them," she said, "in order to flout the population laws."

"Come on," said John Paul. "I've already read the textbook. It's one of the basic principles of community studies. Even people who think they don't want to reproduce still make most of their decisions as if they were active reproducers."

"With exceptions."

"Pathological ones," said John Paul. "You're healthy."

"Are all Polish men as arrogant and intrusive and *rude* as you?"

"Few measure up to my standards, but most try."

"So you decided in class that I was going to be the mother of your children?"

"Theresa," said John Paul, "we're both at prime reproductive age. We both size up everyone we see as potential reproductive partners."

"Maybe I sized you up differently from the way you sized me up."

"I know you did," said John Paul. "But my endeavor for the next while is to make myself irresistible to you."

"Didn't it occur to you that saying it right out loud would be extremely off-putting?"

"Come on," said John Paul. "You knew what I was about from the start. What would I accomplish by pretending?"

"Maybe I want to be courted a little. I have all the needs of an ordinary human female."

"Excuse me," said John Paul, "but some women would think that I was making a pretty damn good start at courting you. You get really bad news, you have a bad phone conversation, you cry in your office, and when you come out, here I am, with comfort food that you know I've gone to a lot of trouble to prepare for you, without your asking – *and* I tell you that I love you and my intention is to be your partner in science, politics, and family-making. I think that's *damned* romantic."

"Well, yes. But something's still missing."

"I know. I was waiting for just the right moment to tell you how much I want to take that ridiculous sweater off of you. I thought I'd wait, though, until you wanted me to do it so badly that you almost couldn't stand it."

She found herself laughing and blushing. "It'll be a long time before *that* happens, buster."

"As long as it takes. I'm a Polish Catholic boy. The kind of girl we marry is the kind that doesn't give you the milk until you buy the cow."

"That's *such* an attractive analogy."

"What about 'Eggs until you buy the chicken'?"

"Try 'Bacon until you buy the pig'?"

"Ouch," he said. "But if you insist, I'll try to think of you in porcine terms."

"You're not going to kiss me tonight."

"Who'd want to? You have salad in your teeth."

"I'm too emotionally on edge to make any kind of rational decision right now."

"I was counting on that."

"And here's a thought," she said. "What if *this* is their plan?"

"Whose plan?"

"Them. The same them we've been talking about. What if the reason they didn't send you back to Poland is because they wanted you to marry a really smart girl – maybe the daughter of the world's leading military theoretician. Of course, they couldn't be sure you'd end up in my section of Human Community."

"Yes, they could," he said thoughtfully.

"Ah," she said. "So you didn't want my section."

He stared at the remnants of the food. "What an interesting idea. We might be somebody's idea of a eugenics program."

"Ever since co-ed colleges began," she said, "it's been a marriage market for people with money to meet and marry people with brains."

"And vice versa."

"But sometimes two people with brains get together."

"And when they have babies, watch out."

Then they both burst out laughing.

"That is way arrogant, even for me," said John Paul. "As if you and I were so valuable that they'd bet the farm on us falling in love with each other."

"Maybe they knew we were both so irresistibly charming that if we ever met, we couldn't help falling in love."

"It's happening to *me*," said John Paul.

"Well, it's not happening to me at all," she said.

"Oh, but I do love a challenge."

"What if we find out that it's true? That they really are pushing us together?"

"So what?" said John Paul. "What does it matter if, by following my heart, I also fulfill someone else's plan?"

"What if we don't like the plan?" she said. "What if this is like Rumpelstiltskin? What if we have to give up what we love best in order to have what we want most?"

"Or vice versa."

"I'm not joking."

"Neither am I," said John Paul. "Even in cultures where marriages are arranged by the parents, you're never actually forbidden to fall in love with your mate."

"I'm not in love, Mr. Wiggin."

"All right then," he said. "Tell me to go away."

She said nothing.

"You aren't telling me to go away."

"I should," she said. "In fact, I already did, several times, and you didn't go."

"I wanted to make sure you knew exactly what you were throwing away. But now that you've eaten my food and heard my confessions, I'm ready to take no for an answer, if you want to say it."

"Well, I'm not going to say it. As long as you understand that *not* saying no doesn't mean yes."

He laughed. "I understand that. I also understand that not saying yes doesn't mean no."

"In some circumstances. About some things."

"So the kiss is still a definite no?" he said.

"I have salad in my teeth, remember?"

He got up onto his knees, leaned over to her, and kissed her lightly on the cheek. "No teeth, no salad," he said.

"I don't even like you yet," she said. "And here you are taking liberties."

He kissed her forehead. "You realize that about three dozen people have seen us sitting here eating. And any one of them might walk by and see me kissing you."

"Scandal," she said.

"Ruin," he said.

"We'll be reported to the authorities," she said.

"It might just make their day," he said.

And since it was an emotional day, and she really did like him, and her feelings were in such a turmoil that she didn't know what was right or good or wise, she yielded to impulse and kissed him back. On the lips. A brief childlike kiss, but a kiss all the same.

Then the mushrooms came, and while John Paul paid for them and tipped the delivery girl, Theresa leaned against the door of her office and tried to think about what had happened today, what was still happening with this Wiggin boy, what might happen in the future, with her career, with her life, with him.

Nothing was clear. Nothing was certain.

And yet, despite all the bad things that had happened and all the tears she had shed, she couldn't help but think that today had been, on balance, a very good day.

ENDER'S GAME

"WHATEVER YOUR GRAVITY IS WHEN YOU GET TO THE door, remember — the enemy's gate is down. If you step through your own door like you're out for a stroll, you're a big target and you deserve to get hit. With more than a flasher." Ender Wiggin paused and looked over the group. Most were just watching him nervously. A few understanding. A few sullen and resisting.

First day with this army, all fresh from the teacher squads, and Ender had forgotten how young new kids could be. He'd been in it for three years, they'd had six months — nobody over nine years old in the whole bunch. But they were his. At eleven, he was half a year early to be a commander. He'd had a toon of his own and knew a few tricks, but there were forty in his new army. Green. All marksmen with a flasher, all in top shape, or they wouldn't be here — but they were all just as likely as not to get wiped out first time into battle.

"Remember," he went on, "they can't see you till you get through that door. But the second you're out, they'll be on you. So hit that door the way you want to be when they shoot at you. Legs up under you, going straight *down*." He pointed at a sullen kid who looked like he was only seven, the smallest of them all. "Which way is down, greenoh!"

"Toward the enemy door." The answer was quick. It was also surly, as if to say, Yeah, yeah, now get on with the important stuff.

"Name, kid?"

"Bean."

"Get that for size or for brains?"

Bean didn't answer. The rest laughed a little. Ender had chosen right. This kid *was* younger than the rest, must have been advanced because he was sharp. The others didn't like him much, they were happy to see him taken down a little. Like Ender's first commander had taken him down.

"Well, Bean, you're right onto things. Now I tell you this, nobody's gonna get through that door without a good chance of getting hit. A lot of you are going to be turned into cement somewhere. Make sure it's your legs. Right? If only your legs get hit, then only your legs get frozen, and in nullo that's no sweat." Ender turned to one of the dazed ones. "What're legs for? Hmmm?"

Blank stare. Confusion. Stammer.

"Forget it. Guess I'll have to ask Bean here."

"Legs are for pushing off walls." Still bored.

"Thanks, Bean. Get that, everybody?" They all got it, and didn't like getting it from Bean. "Right. You can't see with legs, you can't *shoot* with legs, and most of the time they just get in the way. If they get frozen sticking straight out you've turned yourself into a blimp. No way to hide. So how do legs go?"

A few answered this time, to prove that Bean wasn't the only one who knew anything. "Under you. Tucked up under."

"Right. A shield. You're kneeling on a shield, and the shield is your own legs. And there's a trick to the suits. Even when your legs are flashed, you can *still* kick off. I've never seen anybody do it but me – but you're all gonna learn it."

Ender Wiggin turned on his flasher. It glowed faintly green in his hand. Then he let himself rise in the weightless workout room, pulled his legs under him as though he were kneeling, and flashed both of them. Immediately his suit stiffened at the knees and ankles, so that he couldn't bend at all.

"Okay, I'm frozen, see?"

He was floating a meter above them. They all looked up at him, puzzled. He leaned back and caught one of the handholds on the wall behind him, and pulled himself flush against the wall.

"I'm stuck at a wall. If I had legs, I'd use legs, and string myself out like a string *bean*, right?"

They laughed.

"But I don't have legs, and that's *better*, got it? Because of this." Ender jackknifed at the waist, then straightened out violently. He was across the workout room in only a moment. From the other side he called to them. "Got that? I didn't use hands, so I still had use of my flasher. *And* I didn't have my legs floating five feet behind me. Now watch it again."

He repeated the jackknife, and caught a handhold on the wall near them. "Now, I don't just want you to do that when they've flashed your legs. I want you to do that when you've still got legs, because it's better. And because they'll never be expecting it. All right now, everybody up in the air and kneeling."

Most were up in a few seconds. Ender flashed the stragglers, and they dangled, helplessly frozen, while the others laughed. "When I give an order, you move. Got it? When we're at the door and they clear it, I'll be giving you orders in two seconds, as soon as I see the setup. And when I give the order you better be out there, because whoever's out there first is going to win, unless he's a fool. I'm not. And you better not be, or I'll have you back in the teacher squads." He saw more than a few of them gulp, and the frozen ones looked at him with fear. "You guys who are hanging there. You watch. You'll thaw out in about fifteen minutes, and let's see if you can catch up to the others."

For the next half hour Ender had them jackknifing

off walls. He called a stop when he saw that they all had the basic idea. They were a good group, maybe. They'd get better.

"Now you're warmed up," he said to them, "we'll start working."

Ender was the last one out after practice, since he stayed to help some of the slower ones improve on technique. They'd had good teachers, but like all armies they were uneven, and some of them could be a real drawback in battle. Their first battle might be weeks away. It might be tomorrow. A schedule was never posted. The commander just woke up and found a note by his bunk, giving him the time of his battle and the name of his opponent. So for the first while he was going to drive his boys until they were in top shape – all of them. Ready for anything, at any time. Strategy was nice, but it was worth nothing if the soldiers couldn't hold up under the strain.

He turned the corner into the residence wing and found himself face to face with Bean, the seven-year-old he had picked on all through practice that day. Problems. Ender didn't want problems right now.

"Ho, Bean."

"Ho, Ender."

Pause.

"Sir," Ender said softly.

"We're not on duty."

"In my army, Bean, we're always on duty." Ender brushed past him.

Bean's high voice piped up behind him. "I know what you're doing, Ender, sir, and I'm warning you."

Ender turned slowly and looked at him. "Warning me?"

"I'm the best man you've got. But I'd better be treated like it."

"Or what?" Ender smiled menacingly.

"Or I'll be the worst man you've got. One or the other."

"And what do you want? Love and kisses?" Ender was getting angry now.

Bean was unworried. "I want a toon."

Ender walked back to him and stood looking down into his eyes. "I'll give a toon," he said, "to the boys who prove they're worth something. They've got to be good soldiers, they've got to know how to take orders, they've got to be able to think for themselves in a pinch, and they've got to be able to keep respect. That's how I got to be a commander. That's how you'll get to be a toon leader. Got it?"

Bean smiled. "That's fair. *If* you actually work that way, I'll be a toon leader in a month."

Ender reached down and grabbed the front of his uniform and shoved him into the wall. "When I say I work a certain way, Bean, then that's the way I work."

Bean just smiled. Ender let go of him and walked away, and didn't look back. He was sure, without looking, that Bean was still watching, still smiling, still just a little contemptuous. He might make a good toon leader at that. Ender would keep an eye on him.

Captain Graff, six foot two and a little chubby, stroked his belly as he leaned back in his chair. Across his desk sat Lieutenant Anderson, who was earnestly pointing out high points on a chart.

"Here it is, Captain," Anderson said. "Ender's already got them doing a tactic that's going to throw off everyone who meets it. Doubled their speed."

Graff nodded.

"And you know his test scores. He thinks well, too."

Graff smiled. "All true, all true, Anderson, he's a fine student, shows real promise."

They waited.

Graff sighed. "So what do you want me to do?"

"Ender's the one. He's got to be."

"He'll never be ready in time, Lieutenant. He's eleven, for heaven's sake, man, what do you want, a miracle?"

"I want him into battles, every day starting tomorrow. I want him to have a year's worth of battles in a month."

Graff shook his head. "That would be his army in the hospital."

"No, sir. He's getting them into form. And we need Ender."

"Correction, Lieutenant. We need somebody. You think it's Ender."

"All right, I think it's Ender. Which of the commanders if it isn't him?"

"I don't know, Lieutenant." Graff ran his hands over his slightly fuzzy bald head. "These are children, Anderson. Do you realize that? Ender's army is nine years old. Are we going to put them against the older kids? Are we going to put them through hell for a month like that?"

Lieutenant Anderson leaned even farther over Graffs desk.

"Ender's test scores, Captain!"

"I've seen his bloody test scores! I've watched him in battle, I've listened to tapes of his training sessions, I've watched his sleep patterns, I've heard tapes of his conversations in the corridors and in the bathrooms, I'm more aware of Ender Wiggin that you could possibly imagine! And against all the arguments, against his obvious qualities, I'm weighing one thing. I have this picture of Ender a year from now, if you have your way. I see him completely useless, worn down, a failure, because he was pushed farther than he or any living person could go. But it doesn't weigh enough, does it, Lieutenant, because there's a war on, and our best talent is gone, and the biggest battles are ahead. So give Ender a battle every day this week. And then bring me a report."

Anderson stood and saluted. "Thank you, sir."

He had almost reached the door when Graff called his name. He turned and faced the captain.

"Anderson," Captain Graff said. "Have you been outside, lately I mean?"

"Not since last leave, six months ago."

"I didn't think so. Not that it makes any difference. But have you ever been to Beaman Park, there in the city? Hmm? Beautiful park. Trees. Grass. No mallo, no battles, no worries. Do you know what else there is in Beaman Park?"

"What, sir?" Lieutenant Anderson asked.

"Children," Graff answered.

"Of course children," said Anderson.

"I mean children. I mean kids who get up in the morning when their mothers call them and they go to school and then in the afternoons they go to Beaman Park and play. They're happy, they smile a lot, they laugh, they have fun. Hmmm?"

"I'm sure they do, sir."

"Is that all you can say, Anderson?"

Anderson cleared his throat. "It's good for children to have fun, I think, sir. I know I did when I was a boy. But right now the world needs soldiers. And this is the way to get them."

Graff nodded and closed his eyes. "Oh, indeed, you're right, by statistical proof and by all the important theories, and dammit they work and the system is right, but all the same Ender's older than I am. He's not a child. He's barely a person."

"If that's true, sir, then at least we all know that Ender is making it possible for the others of his age to be playing in the park."

"And Jesus died to save all men, of course." Graff sat up and looked at Anderson almost sadly. "But we're the ones," Graff said, "we're the ones who are driving in the nails."

Ender Wiggin lay on his bed staring at the ceiling. He never slept more than five hours a night – but the lights went off at 2200 and didn't come on again until 0600. So he stared at the ceiling and thought.

He'd had his army for three and a half weeks. Dragon Army. The name was assigned, and it wasn't a lucky one. Oh, the charts said that about nine years ago a Dragon Army had done fairly well. But for the next six years the name had been attached to inferior armies, and finally, because of the superstition that was beginning to play about the name, Dragon Army was retired. Until now. And now, Ender thought, smiling, Dragon Army was going to take them by surprise.

The door opened quietly. Ender did not turn his head. Someone stepped softly into his room, then left with the sound of the door shutting. When soft steps died away Ender rolled over and saw a white slip of paper lying on the floor. He reached down and picked it up.

"Dragon Army against Rabbit Army, Ender Wiggin and Carn Carby, 0700."

The first battle. Ender got out of bed and quickly dressed. He went rapidly to the rooms of each of the toon leaders and told them to rouse their boys. In five minutes they were all gathered in the corridor, sleepy and slow. Ender spoke softly.

"First battle, 0700 against Rabbit Army. I've fought them twice before but they've got a new commander. Never heard of him. They're an older group, though, and I knew a few of their olds tricks. Now wake up. Run, doublefast, warmup in workroom three."

For an hour and a half they worked out, with three mock battles and calisthenics in the corridor out of the nullo. Then for fifteen minutes they all lay up in the air, totally relaxing in the weightlessness. At 0650 Ender roused them and they hurried into the corridor. Ender led them down the corridor, running again, and occasionally leaping to touch a light panel on the ceiling. The boys all touched the same light panel. And at 0658 they reached their gate to the battleroom.

The members of toons C and D grabbed the first eight handholds in the ceiling of the corridor. Toons A, B, and E crouched on the floor. Ender hooked his feet into two handholds in the middle of the ceiling, so he was out of everyone's way.

"Which way is the enemy's door?" he hissed.

"Down!" they whispered back, and laughed.

"Flashers on." The boxes in their hands glowed green. They waited for a few seconds more, and then the gray wall in front of them disappeared and the battleroom was visible.

Ender sized it up immediately. The familiar open grid of most early games, like the monkey bars at the park, with seven or eight boxes scattered through the grid. They called the boxes *stars*. There were enough of them, and in forward enough positions, that they were worth going for. Ender decided this in a second, and he hissed, "Spread to near stars. E hold!"

The four groups in the corners plunged through the forcefield at the doorway and fell down into the battleroom. Before the enemy even appeared through the opposite gate Ender's army had spread from the door to the nearest stars.

Then the enemy soldiers came through the door.

From their stance Ender knew they had been in a different gravity, and didn't know enough to disorient themselves from it. They came through standing up, their entire bodies spread and defenseless.

"Kill 'em, E!" Ender hissed, and threw himself out the door knees first, with his flasher between his legs and firing. While Ender's group flew across the room, the rest of Dragon Army lay down a protecting fire, so that E group reached a forward position with only one boy frozen completely, though they had all lost the use of their legs – which didn't impair them in the least. There was a lull as Ender and his opponent, Carn Carby, assessed their positions. Aside from Rabbit Army's losses at the gate, there had been few casualties, and both armies were near full strength. But Carn had no originality – he was in the four-corner spread that any five-year-old in the teacher squads might have thought of. And Ender knew how to defeat it.

He called out, loudly, "E covers A, C·down. B, D angle east wall." Under E toon's cover, B and D toons lunged away from their stars. While they were still exposed, A and C toons left their stars and drifted toward the near wall. They reached it together, and together jackknifed off the wall. At double the normal speed they appeared behind the enemy's stars, and opened fire. In a few seconds the battle was over, with the enemy almost entirely frozen, including the commander, and the rest scattered to the corners. For the next five minutes, in squads of four, Dragon Army cleaned out the dark corners of the battleroom and shepherded the enemy into the center, where their bodies, frozen at impossible angles, jostled each other. Then Ender took three of his boys to the enemy gate and went through the formality of reversing the one-way field by simultaneously touching a Dragon Army helmet at each corner. Then Ender assembled his army in vertical files near the knot of frozen Rabbit Army soldiers.

Only three of Dragon Army's soldiers were immobile. Their victory margin – 38 to 0 – was ridiculously high, and Ender began to laugh. Dragon Army joined him, laughing long and loud. They were still laughing when Lieutenant Anderson and Lieutenant Morris came in from the teachergate at the south end of the battleroom.

Lieutenant Anderson kept his face stiff and unsmiling, but Ender saw him wink as he held out his hand and offered the stiff, formal congratulations that were ritually given to the victor in the game.

Morris found Carn Carby and unfroze him, and the thirteen-year-old came and presented himself to Ender, who laughed without malice and held out his hand. Carn graciously took Ender's hand and bowed his head over it. It was that or be flashed again.

Lieutenant Anderson dismissed Dragon Army, and

they silently left the battleroom through the enemy's
door — again part of the ritual. A light was blinking
on the north side of the square door, indicating where
the gravity was in that corridor. Ender, leading his
soldiers, changed his orientation and went through
the forcefield and into gravity on his feet. His army
followed him at a brisk run back to the workroom.
When they got there they formed up into squads,
and Ender hung in the air, watching them.

"Good first battle," he said, which was excuse
enough for a cheer, which he quieted. "Dragon Army
did all right against Rabbits. But the enemy isn't
always going to be that bad. And if that had been a
good army we would have been smashed. We still
would have won, but we would have been smashed.
Now let me see B and D toons out here. Your take-off
from the stars was way too slow. If Rabbit Army
knew how to aim a flasher, you all would have been
frozen solid before A and C even got to the wall."

They worked out for the rest of the day.

That night Ender went for the first time to the
commanders' mess hall. No one was allowed there
until he had won at least one battle, and Ender was
the youngest commander ever to make it. There was
no great stir when he came in. But when some of the
other boys saw the Dragon on his breast pocket, they
stared at him openly, and by the time he got his tray
and sat at an empty table, the entire room was silent,

with the other commanders watching him. Intensely self-conscious, Ender wondered how they all knew, and why they all looked so hostile.

Then he looked above the door he had just come through. There was a huge scoreboard across the entire wall. It showed the win/loss record for the commander of every army; that day's battles were lit in red. Only four of them. The other three winners had barely made it – the best of them had only two men whole and eleven mobile at the end of the game. Dragon Army's score of thirty-eight mobile was embarrassingly better.

Other new commanders had been admitted to the commanders' mess hall with cheers and congratulations. Other new commanders hadn't won thirty-eight to zero.

Ender looked for Rabbit Army on the scoreboard. He was surprised to find that Carn Carby's score to date was eight wins and three losses. Was he that good? Or had he only fought against inferior armies? Whichever, there was still a zero in Carn's mobile and whole columns, and Ender looked down from the scoreboard grinning. No one smiled back, and Ender knew that they were afraid of him, which meant that they would hate him, which meant that anyone who went into battle against Dragon Army would be scared and angry and less competent. Ender looked for Carn Carby in the crowd, and found him not too far away. He stared at Carby until one of the other boys nudged the Rabbit commander and pointed to Ender. Ender smiled again and waved slightly. Carby turned red, and Ender, satisfied, leaned over his dinner and began to eat.

At the end of the week Dragon Army had fought seven battles in seven days. The score stood seven wins and zero losses. Ender had never had more than five boys frozen in any game. It was no longer possible for the other commanders to ignore Ender. A few of them sat with him and quietly conversed about game strategies that Ender's opponents had used. Other much larger groups were talking with the commanders that Ender had defeated, trying to find out what Ender had done to beat them.

In the middle of the meal the teacher door opened and the groups fell silent as Lieutenant Anderson stepped in and looked over the group. When he located Ender he strode quickly across the room and whispered in Ender's ear. Ender nodded, finished his glass of water, and left with the lieutenant. On the way out, Anderson handed a slip of paper to one of the older boys. The room became very noisy with conversation as Anderson and Ender left.

Ender was escorted down corridors he had never seen before. They didn't have the blue glow of the soldier corridors. Most were wood paneled, and the floors were carpeted. The doors were wood, with nameplates on them, and they stopped at one that said "Captain Graff, supervisor." Anderson knocked softly, and a low voice said, "Come in."

They went in. Captain Graff was seated behind a desk, his hands folded across his potbelly. He nodded, and Anderson sat. Ender also sat down. Graff cleared his throat and spoke.

"Seven days since your first battle, Ender."

Ender did not reply.

"Won seven battles, one every day."

Ender nodded.

"Scores unusually high, too."

Ender blinked.

"Why?" Graff asked him.

Ender glanced at Anderson, and then spoke to the captain behind the desk. "Two new tactics, sir. Legs doubled up as a shield, so that a flash doesn't immobilize. Jackknife takeoffs from the walls. Superior strategy, as Lieutenant Anderson taught, think places, not spaces. Five toons of eight instead of four of ten. Incompetent opponents. Excellent toon leaders, good soldiers."

Graff looked at Ender without expression. Waiting for what, Ender wondered. Lieutenant Anderson spoke up.

"Ender, what's the condition of your army?"

Do they want me to ask for relief? Not a chance, he

decided. "A little tired, in peak condition, morale high, learning fast. Anxious for the next battle."

Anderson looked at Graff. Graff shrugged slightly and turned to Ender.

"Is there anything you want to know?"

Ender held his hands loosely in his lap. "When are you going to put us up against a good army?"

Graff's laughter rang in the room, and when it stopped, Graff handed a piece of paper to Ender. "Now," the captain said, and Ender read the paper. "Dragon Army against Leopard Army, Ender Wiggin and Pol Slattery, 2000."

Ender looked up at Captain Graff. "That's ten minutes from now, sir."

Graff smiled. "Better hurry, then, boy."

As Ender left he realized Pol Slattery was the boy who had been handed his orders as Ender left the mess hall.

He got to his army five minutes later. Three toon leaders were already undressed and lying naked on their beds. He sent them all flying down the corridors to rouse their toons, and gathered up their suits himself. When all his boys were assembled in the corridor, most of them still getting dressed, Ender spoke to them.

"This one's hot and there's no time. We'll be late to the door, and the enemy'll be deployed right outside our gate. Ambush, and I've never heard of it happening before. So we'll take our time at the door. A and B toons, keep your belts loose, and give your flashers to the leaders and seconds of the other toons."

Puzzled, his soldiers complied. By then all were dressed, and Ender led them at a trot to the gate. When they reached it the forcefield was already on one-way, and some of his soldiers were panting. They had had one battle that day and a full workout. They were tired.

Ender stopped at the entrance and looked at the placements of the enemy soldiers. Some of them were grouped not more than twenty feet out from the gate. There was no grid, there were no stars. A big empty space. Where were most of the enemy soldiers? There should have been thirty more.

"They're flat against this wall," Ender said, "where we can't see them."

He took A and B toons and made them kneel, their hands on their hips. Then he flashed them, so that their bodies were frozen rigid.

"You're shields," Ender said, and then had boys from C and D kneel on their legs and hook both arms under the frozen boys' belts. Each boy was holding two flashers. Then Ender and the members of E toon picked up the duos, three at a time, and threw them out the door.

Of course, the enemy opened fire immediately. But

they mainly hit the boys who were already flashed, and in a few moments pandemonium broke out in the battleroom. All the soldiers of Leopard Army were easy targets as they lay pressed flat against the wall or floated, unprotected, in the middle of the battleroom; and Ender's soldiers, armed with two flashers each, carved them up easily. Pol Slattery reacted quickly, ordering his men away from the wall, but not quickly enough – only a few were able to move, and they were flashed before they could get a quarter of the way across the battleroom.

When the battle was over Dragon Army had only twelve boys whole, the lowest score they had ever had. But Ender was satisfied. And during the ritual of surrender Pol Slattery broke form by shaking hands and asking, "Why did you wait so long getting out of the gate?"

Ender glanced at Anderson, who was floating nearby. "I was informed late," he said. "It was an ambush."

Slattery grinned, and gripped Ender's hand again. "Good game."

Ender didn't smile at Anderson this time. He knew that now the games would be arranged against him, to even up the odds. He didn't like it.

It was 2150, nearly time for lights out, when Ender knocked at the door of the room shared by Bean and three other soldiers. One of the others opened the door, then stepped back and held it wide. Ender stood for a moment, then asked if he could come in. They answered, of course, of course, come in, and he walked to the upper bunk, where Bean had set down his book and was leaning on one elbow to look at Ender.

"Bean, can you give me twenty minutes?"

"Near lights out," Bean answered.

"My room," Ender answered. "I'll cover for you."

Bean sat up and slid off his bed. Together he and Ender padded silently down the corridor to Ender's room. Ender entered first, and Bean closed the door behind them.

"Sit down," Ender said, and they both sat on the edge of the bed, looking at each other.

"Remember four weeks ago, Bean? When you told me to make you a toon leader?"

"Yeah."

"I've made five toon leaders since then, haven't I? And none of them was you."

Bean looked at him calmly.

"Was I right?" Ender asked.

"Yes, sir," Bean answered.

Ender nodded. "How have you done in these battles?"

Bean cocked his head to one side. "I've never been immobilized, sir, and I've immobilized forty-three of the enemy. I've obeyed orders quickly, and I've commanded a squad in mop-up and never lost a soldier."

"Then you'll understand this." Ender paused, then decided to back up and say something else first.

"You know you're early, Bean, by a good half year. I was, too, and I've been made a commander six months early. Now they've put me into battles after only three weeks of training with my army. They've given me eight battles in seven days. I've already had more battles than boys who were made commander four months ago. I've won more battles than many who've been commanders for a year. And then tonight. You know what happened tonight."

Bean nodded. "They told you late."

"I don't know what the teachers are doing. But my army is getting tired, and I'm getting tired, and now they're changing the rules of the game. You see, Bean, I've looked in the old charts. No one has ever destroyed so many enemies and kept so many of his own soldiers whole in the history of the game. I'm unique – and I'm getting unique treatment."

Bean smiled. "You're the best, Ender."

Ender shook his head. "Maybe. But it was no accident that I got the soldiers I got. My worst soldier could be a toon leader in another army. I've got the best. They've loaded things my way – but now they're loading it all against me. I don't know why.

But I know I have to be ready for it. I need your help."

"Why mine?"

"Because even though there are some better soldiers than you in Dragon Army – not many, but some – there's nobody who can think better and faster than you." Bean said nothing. They both knew it was true.

Ender continued. "I need to be ready, but I can't retrain the whole army. So I'm going to cut every toon down by one, including you. With four others you'll be a special squad under me. And you'll learn to do some new things. Most of the time you'll be in the regular toons just like you are now. But when I need you. See?"

Bean smiled and nodded. "That's right, that's good, can I pick them myself?"

"One from each toon except your own, and you can't take any toon leaders."

"What do you want us to do?"

"Bean, I don't know. I don't know what they'll throw at us. What would you do if suddenly our flashers didn't work, and the enemy's did? What would you do if we had to face two armies at once? The only thing I know is – there may be a game where we don't even try for score. Where we just go for the enemy's gate. I want you ready to do that any time I call for it. Got it? You take them for two hours a day during regular workout. Then you and I and your soldiers, we'll work at night after dinner."

"We'll get tired."

"I have a feeling we don't know what tired is." Ender reached out and took Bean's hand, and gripped it. "Even when it's rigged against us, Bean. We'll win."

Bean left in silence and padded down the corridor.

Dragon Army wasn't the only army working out after hours now. The other commanders had finally realized they had some catching up to do. From early morning to lights out soldiers all over Training and Command Center, none of them over fourteen years old, were learning to jackknife off walls and use each other as shields.

But while other commanders mastered the techniques that Ender had used to defeat them, Ender and Bean worked on solutions to problems that had never come up.

There were still battles every day, but for a while they were normal, with grids and stars and sudden plunges through the gate. And after the battles, Ender and Bean and four other soldiers would leave the main group and practice strange maneuvers. Attacks without flashers, using feet to physically disarm or disorient an enemy. Using four frozen soldiers to reverse the enemy's gate in less than two seconds. And one day Bean came in to workout with a thirty-meter cord.

"What's that for?"

"I don't know yet." Absently Bean spun one end of the cord. It wasn't more than an eighth of an inch thick, but it would have lifted ten adults without breaking.

"Where did you get it?"

"Commissary. They asked what for. I said to practice tying knots."

Bean tied a loop in the end of the rope and slid it over his shoulders.

"Here, you two, hang on to the wall here. Now don't let go of the rope. Give me about fifty yards of slack." They complied, and Bean moved about ten feet from them along the wall. As soon as he was sure they were ready, he jackknifed off the wall and flew straight out, fifty yards. Then the rope snapped taut. It was so fine that it was virtually invisible, but it was strong enough to force Bean to veer off at almost a right angle. It happened so suddenly that he had inscribed a perfect arc and hit the wall hard before most of the other soldiers knew what had happened. Bean did a perfect rebound and drifted quickly back to where Ender and the others waited for him.

Many of the soldiers in the five regular squads hadn't noticed the rope, and were demanding to know how it was done. It was impossible to change direction that abruptly in nullo. Bean just laughed.

"Wait till the next game without a grid! They'll never know what hit them."

They never did. The next game was only two hours later, but Bean and two others had become pretty good at aiming and shooting while they flew at ridiculous speeds at the end of the rope. The slip of paper was delivered, and Dragon Army trotted off to the gate, to battle with Griffin Army. Bean coiled the rope all the way.

When the gate opened, all they could see was a large brown star only fifteen feet away, completely blocking their view of the enemy's gate.

Ender didn't pause. "Bean, give yourself fifty feet of rope and go around the star." Bean and his four soldiers dropped through the gate and in a moment Bean was launched sideways away from the star. The rope snapped taut, and Bean flew forward. As the rope was stopped by each edge of the star in turn, his arc became tighter and his speed greater, until when he hit the wall only a few feet away from the gate he was barely able to control his rebound to end up behind the star. But he immediately moved all his arms and legs so that those waiting inside the gate would know that the enemy hadn't flashed him anywhere.

Ender dropped through the gate, and Bean quickly

told him how Griffin Army was situated. "They've got two squares of stars, all the way around the gate. All their soldiers are under cover, and there's no way to hit any of them until we're clear to the bottom wall. Even with shields, we'd get there at half strength and we wouldn't have a chance."

"They moving?" Ender asked.

"Do they need to?"

"I would." Ender thought for a moment. "This one's tough. We'll go for the gate, Bean."

Griffin Army began to call out to them.

"Hey, is anybody there?"

"Wake up, there's a war on!"

"We wanna join the picnic!"

They were still calling when Ender's army came out from behind their star with a shield of fourteen frozen soldiers. William Bee, Griffin Army's commander, waited patiently as the screen approached, his men waiting at the fringes of their stars for the moment when whatever was behind the screen became visible. About ten yards away, the screen suddenly exploded as the soldiers behind it shoved the screen north. The momentum carried them south twice as fast, and at the same moment the rest of Dragon Army burst from behind their star at the opposite end of the room, firing rapidly.

William Bee's boys joined battle immediately, of course, but William Bee was far more interested in what had been left behind when the shield disappeared. A formation of four frozen Dragon Army soldiers were moving headfirst toward the Griffin Army gate, held together by another frozen soldier whose feet and hands were hooked through their belts. A sixth soldier hung to the waist and trailed like the tail of a kite. Griffin Army was winning the battle easily, and William Bee concentrated on the formation as it approached the gate. Suddenly the soldier trailing in back moved – he wasn't frozen at all! And even though William Bee flashed him immediately, the damage was done. The format drifted in the Griffin Army gate, and their helmets touched all four corners simultaneously. A buzzer sounded, the gate reversed, and the frozen soldiers in the middle were carried by momentum right through the gate. All the flashers stopped working, and the game was over.

The teachergate opened and Lieutenant Anderson came in. Anderson stopped himself with a slight movement of his hands when he reached the center of the battleroom. "Ender," he called, breaking protocol. One of the frozen Dragon soldiers near the south wall tried to call through jaws that were clamped shut by the suit. Anderson drifted to him and unfroze him.

Ender was smiling.

"I beat you again, sir," Ender said.

Anderson didn't smile. "That's nonsense, Ender,"

Anderson said softly. "Your battle was with William Bee of Griffin Army."

Ender raised an eyebrow.

"After that maneuver," Anderson said, the rules are being revised to require that all of the enemy's soldiers must be immobilized before the gate can be reversed."

"That's all right," Ender said. "It could only work once anyway." Anderson nodded, and was turning away when Ender added, "Is there going to be a new rule that armies be given equal positions to fight from?"

Anderson turned back around. "If you're in one of the positions, Ender, you can hardly call them equal, whatever they are."

William Bee counted carefully and wondered how in the world he had lost when not one of his soldiers had been flashed and only four of Ender's soldiers were even mobile.

And that night as Ender came into the commanders' mess hall, he was greeted with applause and cheers, and his table was crowded with respectful commanders, many of them two or three years older than he was. He was friendly, but while he ate he wondered what the teachers would do to him in his next battle. He didn't need to worry. His next two battles were easy victories, and after that he never saw the battleroom again.

*

It was 2100 and Ender was a little irritated to hear someone knock at his door. His army was exhausted, and he had ordered them all to be in bed after 2030. The last two days had been regular battles, and Ender was expecting the worst in the morning.

It was Bean. He came in sheepishly, and saluted.

Ender returned his salute and snapped. "Bean, I wanted everybody in bed."

Bean nodded but didn't leave. Ender considered ordering him out. But as he looked at Bean, it occurred to him for the first time in weeks just how young Bean was. He had turned eight a week before, and he was still small and – no, Ender thought, he wasn't young. Nobody was young. Bean had been in battle, and with a whole army depending on him he had come through and won. And even though he was small, Ender could never think of him as young again.

Ender shrugged and Bean came over and sat on the edge of the bed. The younger boy looked at his hands for a while, and finally Ender grew impatient and asked, "Well, what is it?"

"I'm transferred. Got orders just a few minutes ago."

Ender closed his eyes for a moment. "I knew they'd pull something new. Now they're taking – where are you going?"

"Rabbit Army."

"How can they put you under an idiot like Carn Carby!"

"Carn was graduated. Support squad."

Ender looked up. "Well, who's commanding Rabbit, then?"

Bean held his hands out helplessly.

"Me," he said.

Ender nodded, and then smiled. "Of course. After all, you're only four years younger than the regular age."

"It isn't funny," Bean said. "I don't know what's going on here. First all the changes in the game. And now this. I wasn't the only one transferred, either, Ender. Ren, Peder, Brian, Wins, Younger. All commanders now."

Ender stood up angrily and strode to the wall. "Every damn toon leader I've got!" he said, and whirled to face Bean. "If they're going to break up my army, Bean, why did they bother making me a commander at all?"

Bean shook his head. "I don't know. You're the best, Ender. Nobody's ever done what you've done. Nineteen battles in fifteen days, sir, and you won every one of them, no matter what they did to you."

"And now you and the others are commanders. You know every trick I've got, I trained you, and who am I supposed to replace you with? Are they going to stick me with six greenohs?"

"It stinks, Ender, but you know that if they gave

you five crippled midgets and armed you with a roll
of toilet paper you'd win."

They both laughed, and then they noticed that
the door was open.

Lieutenant Anderson stepped in. He was followed
by Captain Graff.

"Ender Wiggin," Graff said, holding his hands
across his stomach.

"Yes, sir," Ender answered.

"Orders."

Anderson extended a slip of paper. Ender read it
quickly, then crumpled it, still looking at the air
where the paper had been. After a few minutes he
asked, "Can I tell my army?"

"They'll find out," Graff answered. "It's better not
to talk to them after orders. It makes it easier."

"For you or for me?" Ender asked. He didn't wait
for an answer. He turned quickly to Bean, took his
hand for a moment, and then headed for the door.

"Wait," Bean said. "Where are you going? Tactical
or Support School?"

"Command School," Ender answered, and then he
was gone and Anderson closed the door.

Command School, Bean thought. Nobody went to
Command School until they had gone through three
years of Tactical. But then, nobody went to Tactical
until they had been through at least five years of
Battle School. Ender had only had three.

The system was breaking up. No doubt about it, Bean thought. Either somebody at the top was going crazy, or something was going wrong with the war – the real war, the one they were training to fight in. Why else would they break down the training system, advance somebody – even somebody as good as Ender – straight to Command School? Why else would they ever have an eight-year-old greenoh like Bean command an army?

Bean wondered about it for a long time, and then he finally lay down on Ender's bed and realized that he'd never see Ender again, probably. For some reason that made him want to cry. But he didn't cry, of course. Training in the preschools had taught him how to force down emotions like that. He remembered how his first teacher, when he was three, would have been upset to see his lip quivering and his eyes full of tears.

Bean went through the relaxing routine until he didn't feel like crying anymore. Then he drifted off to sleep. His hand was near his mouth. It lay on his pillow hesitantly, as if Bean couldn't decide whether to bite his nails or suck on his fingertips. His forehead was creased and furrowed. His breathing was quick and light. He was a soldier, and if anyone had asked him what he wanted to be when he grew up, he wouldn't have known what they meant.

*

There's a war on, they said, and that was excuse enough for all the hurry in the world. They said it like a password and flashed a little card at every ticket counter and customs check and guard station. It got them to the head of every line.

Ender Wiggin was rushed from place to place so quickly he had no time to examine anything. But he did see trees for the first time. He saw men who were not in uniform. He saw women. He saw strange animals that didn't speak, but that followed docilely behind women and small children. He saw suitcases and conveyor belts and signs that said words he had never heard of. He would have asked someone what the words meant, except that purpose and authority surrounded him in the persons of four very high officers who never spoke to each other and never spoke to him.

Ender Wiggin was a stranger to the world he was being trained to save. He did not remember ever leaving Battle School before. His earliest memories were of childish war games under the direction of a teacher, of meals with other boys in the gray and green uniforms of the armed forces of his world. He did not know that the gray represented the sky and the green represented the great forests of his planet. All he knew of the world was from vague references to "outside."

And before he could make any sense of the strange

world he was seeing for the first time, they enclosed him again within the shell of the military, where nobody had to say "There's a war on" anymore because no one within the shell of the military forgot it for a single instant of a single day.

They put him in a spaceship and launched him to a large artificial satellite that circled the world.

This space station was called Command School. It held the ansible.

On his first day Ender Wiggin was taught about the ansible and what it meant to warfare. It meant that even though the starships of today's battles were launched a hundred years ago, the commanders of the starships were men of today, who used the ansible to send messages to the computers and the few men on each ship. The ansible sent words as they were spoken, orders as they were made. Battle plans as they were fought. Light was a pedestrian.

For two months Ender Wiggin didn't meet a single person. They came to him namelessly, taught him what they knew, and left him to other teachers. He had no time to miss his friends at Battle School. He only had time to learn how to operate the simulator, which flashed battle patterns around him as if he were in a starship at the center of the battle. How to command mock ships in mock battles by manipulating the keys on the simulator and speaking words into the ansible. How to recognize instantly every enemy ship and the weapons it carried by the pattern that the simulator showed. How to transfer all that he learned in the nullo battles at Battle School to the starship battles at Command School.

He had thought the game was taken seriously before. Here they hurried him through every step, were angry and worried beyond reason every time he forgot something or made a mistake. But he worked as he had always worked, and learned as he had always learned. After a while he didn't make any more mistakes. He used the simulator as if it were a part of himself. Then they stopped being worried and gave him a teacher.

Mazer Rackham was sitting cross-legged on the floor when Ender awoke. He said nothing as Ender got up and showered and dressed, and Ender did not bother to ask him anything. He had long since learned that when something unusual was going on, he would often find out more information faster by waiting than by asking.

Mazer still hadn't spoken when Ender was ready and went to the door to leave the room. The door didn't open. Ender turned to face the man sitting on the floor. Mazer was at least forty, which made him the oldest man Ender had ever seen close up. He had a day's growth of black and white whiskers that grizzled his face only slightly less than his close-cut hair.

His face sagged a little and his eyes were surrounded by creases and lines. He looked at Ender without interest.

Ender turned back to the door and tried again to open it.

"All right," he said, giving up. "Why's the door locked?"

Mazer continued to look at him blankly.

Ender became impatient. "I'm going to be late. If I'm not supposed to be there until later, then tell me so I can go back to bed." No answer. "Is it a guessing game?" Ender asked. No answer. Ender decided that maybe the man was trying to make him angry, so he went through a relaxing exercise as he leaned on the door, and soon he was calm again. Mazer didn't take his eyes off Ender.

For the next two hours the silence endured. Mazer watching Ender constantly, Ender trying to pretend he didn't notice the old man. The boy became more and more nervous, and finally ended up walking from one end of the room to the other in a sporadic pattern.

He walked by Mazer as he had several times before, and Mazer's hand shot out and pushed Ender's left leg into his right in the middle of a step. Ender fell flat on the floor.

He leaped to his feet immediately, furious. He found Mazer sitting calmly, cross-legged, as if he had never moved. Ender stood poised to fight. But the man's immobility made it impossible for Ender to attack, and he found himself wondering if he had only imagined the old man's hand tripping him up.

The pacing continued for another hour, with Ender Wiggin trying the door every now and then. At last he gave up and took off his uniform and walked to his bed.

As he leaned over to pull the covers back, he felt a hand jab roughly between his thighs and another hand grab his hair. In a moment he had been turned upside down. His face and shoulders were being pressed into the floor by the old man's knee, while his back was excruciatingly bent and his legs were pinioned by Mazer's arm. Ender was helpless to use his arms, and he couldn't bend his back to gain slack so he could use his legs. In less than two seconds the old man had completely defeated Ender Wiggin.

"All right," Ender gasped. "You win."

Mazer's knee thrust painfully downward.

"Since when," Mazer asked in a soft, rasping voice, "do you have to tell the enemy when he has won?"

Ender remained silent.

"I surprised you once, Ender Wiggin. Why didn't you destroy me immediately? Just because I looked peaceful? You turned your back on me. Stupid. You have learned nothing. You have never had a teacher."

Ender was angry now. "I've had too many damned

teachers, how was I supposed to know you'd turn out to be a –" Ender hunted for the word. Mazer supplied one.

"An enemy, Ender Wiggin," Mazer whispered. "I am your enemy, the first one you've ever had who was smarter than you. There is no teacher but the enemy, Ender Wiggin. No one but the enemy will ever tell you what the enemy is going to do. No one but the enemy will ever teach you how to destroy and conquer. I am your enemy, from now on. From now on I am your teacher."

Then Mazer let Ender's legs fall to the floor. Because the old man still held Ender's head to the floor, the boy couldn't use his arms to compensate, and his legs hit the plastic surface with a loud crack and a sickening pain that made Ender wince. Then Mazer stood and let Ender rise.

Slowly the boy pulled his legs under him, with a faint groan of pain, and he knelt on all fours for a moment, recovering. Then his right arm flashed out. Mazer quickly danced back and Ender's hand closed on air as his teacher's foot shot forward to catch Ender on the chin.

Ender's chin wasn't there. He was lying flat on his back, spinning on the floor, and during the moment that Mazer was off balance from his kick Ender's feet smashed into Mazer's other leg. The old man fell on the ground in a heap.

What seemed to be a heap was really a hornet's nest. Ender couldn't find an arm or a leg that held still long enough to be grabbed, and in the meantime blows were landing on his back and arms. Ender was smaller – he couldn't reach past the old man's flailing limbs.

So he leaped back out of the way and stood poised near the door.

The old man stopped thrashing about and sat up, cross-legged again, laughing. "Better, this time, boy. But slow. You will have to be better with a fleet than you are with your body or no one will be safe with you in command. Lesson learned?"

Ender nodded slowly.

Mazer smiled. "Good. Then we'll never have such a battle again. All the rest with the simulator. I will program your battles, I will devise the strategy of your enemy, and you will learn to be quick and discover what tricks the enemy has for you. Remember, boy. From now on the enemy is more clever than you. From now on the enemy is stronger than you. From now on you are always about to lose."

Then Mazer's face became serious again. "You will be about to lose, Ender, but you will win. You will learn to defeat the enemy. He will teach you how."

Mazer got up and walked to the door. Ender stepped out of the way. As the old man touched the handle of the door, Ender leaped into the air and kicked Mazer in the small of the back with both feet. He hit hard enough that he rebounded onto his feet, as Mazer cried out and collapsed on the floor.

Mazer got up slowly, holding on to the door handle, his face contorted with pain. He seemed disabled, but Ender didn't trust him. He waited warily. And yet in spite of his suspicion he was caught off guard by Mazer's speed. In a moment he found himself on the floor near the opposite wall, his nose and lip bleeding where his face had hit the bed. He was able to turn enough to see Mazer open the door and leave. The old man was limping and walking slowly.

Ender smiled in spite of the pain, then rolled over onto his back and laughed until his mouth filled with blood and he started to gag. Then he got up and painfully made his way to his bed. He lay down and in a few minutes a medic came and took care of his injuries.

As the drug had its effect and Ender drifted off to sleep he remembered the way Mazer limped out of his room and laughed again. He was still laughing softly as his mind went blank and the medic pulled the blanket over him and snapped off the light. He slept until pain woke him in the morning. He dreamed of defeating Mazer.

The next day Ender went to the simulator room with his nose bandaged and his lip still puffy. Mazer was not there. Instead, a captain who had worked with him before showed him an addition that had been made. The captain pointed to a tube with a loop at one end. "Radio. Primitive, I know, but it loops over your ear and we tuck the other end into your mouth like this."

"Watch it," Ender said as the captain pushed the end of the tube into his swollen lip.

"Sorry. Now you just talk."

"Good. Who to?"

The captain smiled. "Ask and see."

Ender shrugged and turned to the simulator. As he did a voice reverberated through his skull. It was too loud for him to understand, and he ripped the radio off his ear.

"What are you trying to do, make me deaf?"

The captain shook his head and turned a dial on a small box on a nearby table. Ender put the radio back on.

"Commander," the radio said in a familiar voice.

Ender answered, "Yes."

"Instructions, sir?"

The voice was definitely familiar. "Bean?" Ender asked.

"Yes, sir."

"Bean, this is Ender."

Silence. And then a burst of laughter from the other side. Then six or seven more voices laughing, and Ender waited for silence to return. When it did, he asked, "Who else?"

A few voices spoke at once, but Bean drowned them out. "Me, I'm Bean, and Peder, Wins, Younger, Lee, and Vlad."

Ender thought for a moment. Then he asked what the hell was going on. They laughed again.

"They can't break up the group," Bean said. "We were commanders for maybe two weeks, and here we are at Command School, training with the simulator, and all of a sudden they told us we were going to form a fleet with a new commander. And that's you."

Ender smiled. "Are you boys any good?"

"If we aren't, you'll let us know."

Ender chuckled a little. "Might work out. A fleet."

For the next ten days Ender trained his toon leaders until they could maneuver their ships like precision dancers. It was like being back in the battleroom again, except that now Ender could always see everything, and could speak to his toon leaders and change their orders at any time.

One day as Ender sat down at the control board and switched on the simulator, harsh green lights appeared in the space – the enemy.

"This is it," Ender said. "X, Y, bullet, C, D, reserve screen, E, south loop, Bean, angle north."

The enemy was grouped in a globe, and outnumbered Ender two to one. Half of Ender's force was grouped in a tight, bulletlike formation, with the rest in a flat circular screen – except for a tiny force under Bean that moved off the simulator, heading behind the enemy's formation. Ender quickly learned the enemy's strategy: whenever Ender's bullet formation came close, the enemy would give way, hoping to draw Ender inside the globe where he would be surrounded. So Ender obligingly fell into the trap, bringing his bullet to the center of the globe.

The enemy began to contract slowly, not wanting to come within range until all their weapons could be brought to bear at once. Then Ender began to work in earnest. His reserve screen approached the outside of the globe, and the enemy began to concentrate his forces there. Then Bean's force appeared on the opposite side, and the enemy again deployed ships on that side.

Which left most of the globe only thinly defended. Ender's bullet attacked, and since at the point of attack it outnumbered the enemy overwhelmingly, he tore a hole in the formation. The enemy reacted to try to plug the gap, but in the confusion the reserve force and Bean's small force attacked simultaneously, while the bullet moved to another part of the globe. In a few more minutes the formation was shattered, most of the enemy ships destroyed, and the few survivors rushing away as fast as they could go.

Ender switched the simulator off. All the lights faded. Mazer was standing beside Ender, his hands in his pockets, his body tense. Ender looked up at him.

"I thought you said the enemy would be smart," Ender said.

Mazer's face remained expressionless. "What did you learn?"

"I learned that a sphere only works if your enemy's a fool. He had his forces so spread out that I outnumbered him whenever I engaged him."

"And?"

"And," Ender said, "you can't stay committed to one pattern. It makes you too easy to predict."

"Is that all?" Mazer asked quietly.

Ender took off his radio. "The enemy could have defeated me by breaking the sphere earlier."

Mazer nodded. "You had an unfair advantage."

Ender looked up at him coldly. "I was outnumbered two to one."

Mazer shook his head. "You have the ansible. The enemy doesn't. We include that in the mock battles. Their messages travel at the speed of light."

Ender glanced toward the simulator. "Is there enough space to make a difference?"

"Don't you know?" Mazer asked. "None of the ships was ever closer than thirty thousand kilometers to any other."

Ender tried to figure the size of the enemy's

sphere. Astronomy was beyond him. But now his curiosity was stirred.

"What kind of weapons are on those ships? To be able to strike so fast?"

Mazer shook his head. "The science is too much for you. You'd have to study many more years than you've lived to understand even the basics. All you need to know is that the weapons work."

"Why do we have to come so close to be in range?"

"The ships are all protected by forcefields. A certain distance away the weapons are weaker and can't get through. Closer in the weapons are stronger than the shields. But the computers take care of all that. They're constantly firing in any direction that won't hurt one of our ships. The computers pick targets, aim; they do all the detail work. You just tell them when and get them in a position to win. All right?"

"No," Ender twisted the tube of the radio around his fingers. "I have to know how the weapons work."

"I told you, it would take —"

"I can't command a fleet — not even on the simulator — unless I know." Ender waited a moment, then added, "Just the rough idea."

Mazer stood up and walked a few steps away. "All right, Ender. It won't make any sense, but I'll try. As simply as I can." He shoved his hands into his pockets. "It's this way, Ender. Everything is made up of atoms, little particles so small you can't see them with your eyes. These atoms, there are only a few different types, and they're all made up of even smaller particles that are pretty much the same. These atoms can be broken, so that they stop being atoms. So that this metal doesn't hold together anymore. Or the plastic floor. Or your body. Or even the air. They just seem to disappear, if you break the atoms. All that's left is the pieces. And they fly around and break more atoms. The weapons on the ships set up an area where it's impossible for atoms of anything to stay together. They all break down. So things in that area – they disappear."

Ender nodded. "You're right, I don't understand it. Can it be blocked?"

"No. But it gets wider and weaker the farther it goes from the ship, so that after a while a forcefield will block it. OK? And to make it strong at all, it has to be focused so that a ship can only fire effectively in maybe three or four directions at once."

Ender nodded again, but he didn't really understand, not well enough. "If the pieces of the broken atoms go breaking more atoms, why doesn't it just make everything disappear?"

"Space. Those thousands of kilometers between the ships, they're empty. Almost no atoms. The pieces don't hit anything, and when they finally do hit something, they're so spread out they can't do any harm." Mazer cocked his head quizzically. "Anything else you need to know?"

"Do the weapons on the ships – do they work against anything besides ships?"

Mazer moved in close to Ender and said firmly, "We only use them against ships. Never anything else. If we used them against anything else, the enemy would use them against us. Got it?"

Mazer walked away, and was nearly out the door when Ender called to him.

"I don't know your name yet," Ender said blandly.

"Mazer Rackham."

"Mazer Rackham," Ender said, "I defeated you."

Mazer laughed.

"Ender, you weren't fighting me today," he said. "You were fighting the stupidest computer in the Command School, set on a ten-year-old program. You don't think I'd use a sphere, do you?" He shook his head. "Ender, my dear little fellow, when you fight me, you'll know it. Because you'll lose." And Mazer left the room.

Ender still practiced ten hours a day with his toon leaders. He never saw them, though, only heard their voices on the radio. Battles came every two or three days. The enemy had something new every time, something harder – but Ender coped with it. And won every time. And after every battle Mazer would point out mistakes and show Ender that he had really lost. Mazer only let Ender finish so that he would learn to handle the end of the game.

Until finally Mazer came in and solemnly shook Ender's hand and said, "That, boy, was a good battle."

Because the praise was so long in coming, it pleased Ender more than praise had ever pleased him before. And because it was so condescending, he resented it.

"So from now on," Mazer said, "we can give you hard ones.

From then on Ender's life was a slow nervous breakdown.

He began fighting two battles a day, with problems that steadily grew more difficult. He had been trained in nothing but the game all his life, but now the game began to consume him. He woke in the morning with new strategies for the simulator and went fitfully to sleep at night with the mistakes of the day preying on him. Sometimes he would wake up in the middle of the night crying for a reason he didn't remember. Sometimes he woke up with his knuckles bloody from biting them. But every day he went impassively to the simulator and drilled his toon leaders until the battles, and drilled his toon leaders after the battles, and endured and studied the harsh criticism that Rackham piled on him. He noted that Rackham perversely criticized him more after his hardest battles. He noted that every time he thought of a new strategy the enemy was using it within a few days. And he noted that while his fleet always stayed the same size, the enemy increased in numbers every day.

He asked his teacher.

"We are showing you what it will be like when you really command. The ratios of enemy to us."

"Why does the enemy always outnumber us?"

Mazer bowed his gray head for a moment, as if deciding whether to answer. Finally he looked up and reached out his hand and touched Ender on the shoulder. "I will tell you, even though the information is secret. You see, the enemy attacked us first. He had good reason to attack us, but that is a matter for politicians, and whether the fault was ours or his, we could not let him win. So when the enemy came to our worlds, we fought back, hard, and spent the finest of our young men in the fleets. But we won, and the enemy retreated."

Mazer smiled ruefully. "But the enemy was not through, boy. The enemy would never be through. They came again, with more numbers, and it was harder to beat them. And another generation of young men was spent. Only a few survived. So we came up with a plan – the big men came up with the plan. We knew that we had to destroy the enemy once and for all, totally, eliminate his ability to make war against us. To do that we had to go to his home worlds – his home world, really, since the enemy's empire is all tied to his capital world."

"And so?" Ender asked.

"And so we made a fleet. We made more ships than the enemy ever had. We made a hundred ships for every ship he had sent against us. And we launched them against his twenty-eight worlds. They started leaving a hundred years ago. And they carried on them the ansible, and only a few men. So that someday a commander could sit on a planet somewhere far from the battle and command the fleet. So that our best minds would not be destroyed by the enemy."

Ender's questions had still not been answered. "Why do they outnumber us?"

Mazer laughed. "Because it took a hundred years for our ships to get there. They've had a hundred years to prepare for us. They'd be fools, don't you think, boy, if they waited in old tugboats to defend their harbors. They have new ships, great ships, hundreds of ships. All we have is the ansible, that and the fact that they have to put a commander with every fleet, and when they lose – and they will lose – they lose one of their best minds every time."

Ender started to ask another question.

"No more, Ender Wiggin. I've told you more than you ought to know as it is."

Ender stood angrily and turned away. "I have a right to know. Do you think this can go on forever, pushing me through one school and another and never telling me what my life is for? You use me and the others as a tool, someday we'll command your ships, someday maybe we'll save your lives, but I'm not a computer, and I have to *know*!"

"Ask me a question, then, boy," Mazer said, "and if I can answer, I will."

"If you use your best minds to command the fleets, and you never lose any, then what do you need me for? Who am I replacing, if they're all still there?"

Mazer shook his head. "I can't tell you the answer to that, Ender. Be content that we will need you, soon. It's late. Go to bed. You have a battle in the morning."

Ender walked out of the simulator room. But when Mazer left by the same door a few moments later, the boy was waiting in the hall.

"All right, boy," Mazer said impatiently, 'what is it? I don't have all night and you need to sleep."

Ender wasn't sure what his question was, but Mazer waited. Finally Ender asked softly, "Do they live?"

"Do who live?"

"The other commanders. The ones now. And before me."

Mazer snorted. "Live. Of course they live. He

wonders if they live." Still chuckling, the old man walked off down the hall. Ender stood in the corridor for a while, but at last he was tired and he went off to bed. They live, he thought. They live, but he can't tell me what happens to them.

That night Ender didn't wake up crying. But he did wake up with blood on his hands.

Months wore on with battles every day, until at last Ender settled into the routine of the destruction of himself. He slept less every night, dreamed more, and he began to have terrible pains in his stomach. They put him on a very bland diet, but soon he didn't even have an appetite for that. "Eat," Mazer said, and Ender would mechanically put food in his mouth. But if nobody told him to eat he didn't eat.

One day as he was drilling his toon leaders the room went black and he woke up on the floor with his face bloody where he had hit the controls.

They put him to bed then, and for three days he was very ill. He remembered seeing faces in his dreams, but they weren't real faces, and he knew it even while he thought he saw them. He thought he saw Bean sometimes, and sometimes he thought he saw Lieutenant Anderson and Captain Graff. And then he woke up and it was only his enemy, Mazer Rackham.

"I'm awake," he said to Mazer Rackham.

"So I see," Mazer answered. "Took you long enough. You have a battle today."

So Ender got up and fought the battle and he won it. But there was no second battle that day, and they let him go to bed earlier. His hands were shaking as he undressed.

During the night he thought he felt hands touching him gently, and he dreamed he heard voices saying, "How long can he go on?"

"Long enough."

"So soon?"

"In a few days, then he's through."

"How will he do?"

"Fine. Even today, he was better than ever."

Ender recognized the last voice as Mazer Rackham's. He resented Rackham's intruding even in his sleep.

He woke up and fought another battle and won.

Then he went to bed.

He woke up and won again.

And the next day was his last day in Command School, though he didn't know it. He got up and went to the simulator for the battle.

Mazer was waiting for him. Ender walked slowly into the simulator room. His step was slightly shuffling, and he seemed tired and dull. Mazer frowned.

"Are you awake, boy?" If Ender had been alert, he

would have cared more about the concern in his teacher's voice. Instead, he simply went to the controls and sat down. Mazer spoke to him.

"Today's game needs a little explanation, Ender Wiggin. Please turn around and pay strict attention."

Ender turned around, and for the first time he noticed that there were people at the back of the room. He recognized Graff and Anderson from Battle School, and vaguely remembered a few of the men from Command School — teachers for a few hours at some time or another. But most of the people he didn't know at all.

"Who are they?"

Mazer shook his head and answered, "Observers. Every now and then we let observers come in to watch the battle. If you don't want them, we'll send them out."

Ender shrugged. Mazer began his explanation. "Today's game, boy, has a new element. We're staging this battle around a planet. This will complicate things in two ways. The planet isn't large, on the scale we're using, but the ansible can't detect anything on the other side of it — so there's a blind spot. Also, it's against the rules to use weapons against the planet itself. All right?"

"Why, don't the weapons work against planets?"

Mazer answered coldly, "There are rules of war, Ender, that apply even in training games."

Ender shook his head slowly. "Can the planet attack?"

Mazer looked nonplussed for a moment, then smiled. "I guess you'll have to find that one out, boy. And one more thing. Today, Ender, your opponent isn't the computer. I am your enemy today, and today I won't be letting you off so easily. Today is a battle to the end. And I'll use any means I can to defeat you."

Then Mazer was gone, and Ender expressionlessly led his toon leaders through maneuvers. Ender was doing well, of course, but several of the observers shook their heads, and Graff kept clasping and unclasping his hands, crossing and uncrossing his legs. Ender would be slow today, and today Ender couldn't afford to be slow.

A warning buzzer sounded, and Ender cleared the simulator board, waiting for today's game to appear. He felt muddled today, and wondered why people were there watching. Were they going to judge him today? Decide if he was good enough for something else? For another two years of grueling training, another two years of struggling to exceed his best? Ender was twelve. He felt very old. And as he waited for the game to appear, he wished he could simply lose it, lose the battle badly and completely so that they would remove him from the program, punish him however they wanted, he didn't care, just so he could sleep.

Then the enemy formation appeared, and Ender's weariness turned to desperation.

The enemy outnumbered them a thousand to one, the simulator glowed green with them, and Ender knew that he couldn't win.

And the enemy was not stupid. There was no formation that Ender could study and attack. Instead the vast swarms of ships were constantly moving, constantly shifting from one momentary formation to another, so that a space that for one moment was empty was immediately filled with a formidable enemy force. And even though Ender's fleet was the largest he had ever had, there was no place he could deploy it where he would outnumber the enemy long enough to accomplish anything.

And behind the enemy was the planet. The planet, which Mazer had warned him about. What difference did a planet make, when Ender couldn't hope to get near it? Ender waited, waited for the flash of insight that would tell him what to do, how to destroy the enemy. And as he waited, he heard the observers behind him begin to shift in their seats, wondering what Ender was doing, what plan he would follow. And finally it was obvious to everyone that Ender didn't know what to do, that there was nothing to do, and a few of the men at the back of the room made quiet little sounds in their throats.

Then Ender heard Bean's voice in his ear. Bean

chuckled and said, "Remember, the enemy's gate is *down*." A few of the other toon leaders laughed, and Ender thought back to the simple games he had played and won in Battle School. They had put him against hopeless odds there, too. And he had beaten them. And he'd be damned if he'd let Mazer Rackham beat him with a cheap trick like outnumbering him a thousand to one. He had won a game in Battle School by going for something the enemy didn't expect, something against the rules — he had won by going against the enemy's gate.

And the enemy's gate was down.

Ender smiled, and realized that if he broke this rule they'd probably kick him out of school, and that way he'd win for sure. He would never have to play a game again.

He whispered into the microphone. His six commanders each took a part of the fleet and launched themselves against the enemy. They pursued erratic courses, darting off in one direction and then another. The enemy immediately stopped his aimless maneuvering and began to group around Ender's six fleets.

Ender took off his microphone, leaned back in his chair, and watched. The observers murmured out loud, now. Ender was doing nothing — he had thrown the game away.

But a pattern began to emerge from the quick confrontations with the enemy. Ender's six groups lost ships constantly as they brushed with each enemy force – but they never stopped for a fight, even when for a moment they could have won a small tactical victory. Instead they continued on their erratic course that led, eventually, down. Toward the enemy planet.

And because of their seemingly random course the enemy didn't realize it until the same time that the observers did. By then it was too late, just as it had been too late for William Bee to stop Ender's soldiers from activating the gate. More of Ender's ships could be hit and destroyed, so that of the six fleets only two were able to get to the planet, and those were decimated. But those tiny groups *did* get through, and they opened fire on the planet.

Ender leaned forward now, anxious to see if his guess would pay off. He half expected a buzzer to sound and the game to be stopped, because he had broken the rule. But he was betting on the accuracy of the simulator. If it could simulate a planet, it could simulate what would happen to a planet under attack.

It did.

The weapons that blew up little ships didn't blow up the entire planet at first. But they did cause terrible explosions. And on the planet there was no space to dissipate the chain reaction. On the planet the chain reaction found more and more fuel to feed it.

The planet's surface seemed to be moving back

and forth, but soon the surface gave way to an immense explosion that sent light flashing in all directions. It swallowed up Ender's entire fleet. And then it reached the enemy ships.

The first simply vanished in the explosion. Then, as the explosion spread and became less bright, it was clear what happened to each ship. As the light reached them they flashed brightly for a moment and disappeared. They were all fuel for the fire of the planet.

It took more than three minutes for the explosion to reach the limits of the simulator, and by then it was much fainter. All the ships were gone, and if any had escaped before the explosion reached them, they were few and not worth worrying about. Where the planet had been there was nothing. The simulator was empty.

Ender had destroyed the enemy by sacrificing his entire fleet and breaking the rule against destroying the enemy planet. He wasn't sure whether to feel triumphant at his victory or defiant at the rebuke he was certain would come. So instead he felt nothing. He was tired. He wanted to go to bed and sleep.

He switched off the simulator, and finally heard the noise behind him.

There were no longer two rows of dignified military observers. Instead there was chaos. Some of them were slapping each other on the back, some of them were bowed, head in hands, others were openly weeping. Captain Graff detached himself from the group and came to Ender. Tears streamed down his face, but he was smiling. He reached out his arms, and to Ender's surprise he embraced the boy, held him tightly, and whispered, "Thank you, thank you, thank you, Ender."

Soon all the observers were gathered around the bewildered child, thanking him and cheering him and patting him on the shoulder and shaking his hand. Ender tried to make sense of what they were saying. Had he passed the test after all? Why did it matter so much to them?

Then the crowd parted and Mazer Rackham walked through. He came straight up to Ender Wiggin and held out his hand.

"You made the hard choice, boy. But heaven knows there was no other way you could have done it. Congratulations. You beat them, and it's all over."

All over. Beat them. "I beat you, Mazer Rackham."

Mazer laughed, a loud laugh that filled the room. "Ender Wiggin, you never played me. You never played a *game* since I was your teacher."

Ender didn't get the joke. He had played a great many games, at a terrible cost to himself. He began to get angry.

Mazer reached out and touched his shoulder. Ender shrugged him off. Mazer then grew serious and said,

"Ender Wiggin, for the last months you have been the commander of our fleets. There were no games. The battles were real. Your only enemy was *the* enemy. You won every battle. And finally today you fought them at their home world, and you destroyed their world, their fleet, you destroyed them completely, and they'll never come against us again. You did it. You."

Real. Not a game. Ender's mind was too tired to cope with it all. He walked away from Mazer, walked silently through the crowd that still whispered thanks and congratulations to the boy, walked out of the simulator room and finally arrived in his bedroom and closed the door.

He was asleep when Graff and Mazer Rackham found him. They came in quietly and roused him. He awoke slowly, and when he recognized them he turned away to go back to sleep.

"Ender," Graff said. "We need to talk to you."

Ender rolled back to face them. He said nothing.

Graff smiled. "It was a shock to you yesterday, I know. But it must make you feel good to know you won the war."

Ender nodded slowly.

"Mazer Rackham here, he never played against you. He only analyzed your battles to find out your weak spots, to help you improve. It worked, didn't it?"

Ender closed his eyes tightly. They waited. He said, "Why didn't you tell me?"

Mazer smiled. "A hundred years ago, Ender, we found out some things. That when a commander's life is in danger he becomes afraid, and fear slows down his thinking. When a commander knows that he's killing people, he becomes cautious or insane, and neither of those help him do well. And when he's mature, when he has responsibilities and an understanding of the world, he becomes cautious and sluggish and can't do his job. So we trained children, who didn't know anything but the game, and never knew when it would become real. That was the theory, and you proved that the theory worked."

Graff reached out and touched Ender's shoulder. "We launched the ships so that they would all arrive at their destination during these few months. We knew that we'd probably have only one good commander, if we were lucky. In history it's been very rare to have more than one genius in a war. So we planned on having a genius. We were gambling. And you came along and we won."

Ender opened his eyes again and they realized that he was angry. "Yes, you won."

Graff and Mazer Rackham looked at each other. "He doesn't understand," Graff whispered.

"I understand," Ender said. "You needed a weapon, and you got it, and it was me."

"That's right," Mazer answered.

"So tell me," Ender went on, "how many people lived on that planet that I destroyed."

They didn't answer him. They waited awhile in silence, and then Graff spoke. "Weapons don't need to understand what they're pointed at, Ender. We did the pointing, and so we're responsible. You just did your job."

Mazer smiled. "Of course, Ender, you'll be taken care of. The government will never forget you. You served us all very well."

Ender rolled over and faced the wall, and even though they tried to talk to him, he didn't answer them. Finally they left.

Ender lay in his bed for a long time before anyone disturbed him again. The door opened softly. Ender didn't turn to see who it was. Then a hand touched him softly.

"Ender, it's me, Bean."

Ender turned over and looked at the little boy who was standing by his bed.

"Sit down," Ender said.

Bean sat. "That last battle, Ender. I didn't know how you'd get us out of it."

Ender smiled. "I didn't. I cheated. I thought they'd kick me out."

"Can you believe it! We won the war. The whole war's over, and we thought we'd have to wait till we grew up to fight in it, and it was us fighting it all the time. I mean, Ender, we're little kids. I'm a little kid, anyway." Bean laughed and Ender smiled. Then they were silent for a little while, Bean sitting on the edge of the bed, Ender watching him out of half-closed eyes.

Finally Bean thought of something else to say.

"What will we do now that the war's over?" he said.

Ender closed his eyes and said, "I need some sleep, Bean."

Bean got up and left and Ender slept.

Graff and Anderson walked through the gates into the park. There was a breeze, but the sun was hot on their shoulders.

"Abba Technics? In the capital?" Graff asked.

"No, in Biggock County. Training division," Anderson replied. "They think my work with children is good preparation. And you?"

Graff smiled and shook his head. "No plans. I'll be here for a few more months. Reports, winding down. I've had offers. Personnel development for DCIA, executive vice-president for U and P, but I said no. Publisher wants me to do memoirs of the war. I don't know."

They sat on a bench and watched leaves shivering in the breeze. Children on the monkey bars were laughing and yelling, but the wind and the distance swallowed their words. "Look," Graff said, pointing. A little boy jumped from the bars and ran near the bench where the two men sat. Another boy followed him, and holding his hands like a gun he made an explosive sound. The child he was shooting at didn't stop. He fired again.

"I got you! Come back here!"

The other little boy ran on out of sight.

"Don't you know when you're dead?" The boy shoved his hands in his pockets and kicked a rock back to the monkey bars. Anderson smiled and shook his head. "Kids," he said. Then he and Graff stood up and walked on out of the park.

INVESTMENT COUNSELOR

ANDREW WIGGIN TURNED TWENTY THE DAY HE REACHED the planet Sorelledolce. Or rather, after complicated calculations of how many seconds he had been in flight, and at what percentage of lightspeed, and therefore what amount of subjective time had elapsed for him, he reached the conclusion that he had passed his twentieth birthday just before the end of the voyage.

This was much more relevant to him than the other pertinent fact – that four hundred and some-odd years had passed since the day he was born, back on Earth, back when the human race had not spread beyond the solar system of its birth.

When Valentine emerged from the debarkation chamber – alphabetically she was always after him – Andrew greeted her with the news. "I just figured it out," he said. "I'm twenty."

"Good," she said. "Now you can start paying taxes like the rest of us."

Ever since the end of the War of Xenocide, Andrew had lived on a trust fund set up by a grateful world to reward the commander of the fleets that saved humanity. Well, strictly speaking, that action was taken at the end of the Third Bugger War, when people still thought of the Buggers as monsters and the children who commanded the fleet as heroes. By the time the name was changed to the War of Xenocide, humanity was no longer grateful, and the last thing any government would have dared to do was authorize a pension trust fund for Ender Wiggin, the perpetrator of the most awful crime in human history.

In fact, if it had become known that such a trust fund existed, it would have become a public scandal. But the interstellar fleet was slow to convert to the idea that destroying the Buggers had been a bad idea. And so they carefully shielded the trust fund from public view, dispersing it among many mutual funds and as stock in many different companies, with no single authority controlling any significant portion of the money. Effectively, they had made the money disappear, and only Andrew himself and his sister Valentine knew where the money was, or how much of it there was.

One thing, though, was certain: By law, when Andrew reached the subjective age of twenty, the tax-exempt status of his holdings would be revoked. The income would start being reported to the appropriate authorities. Andrew would have to file a tax report either every year or every time he concluded an inter-stellar voyage of greater than one year in objective time, the taxes to be annualized and interest on the unpaid portion duly handed over.

Andrew was not looking forward to it.

"How does it work with your book royalties?" he asked Valentine.

"The same as anyone," she answered, "except that not many copies sell, so there isn't much in the way of taxes to pay."

Only a few minutes later she had to eat her words, for when they sat down at the rental computers in the starport of Sorelledolce, Valentine discovered that her most recent book, a history of the failed Jung and Calvin colonies on the planet Helvetica, had achieved something of a cult status.

"I think I'm rich," she murmured to Andrew.

"I have no idea whether I'm rich or not," said Andrew. "I can't get the computer to stop listing my holdings."

The names of companies kept scrolling up and back, the list going on and on.

"I thought they'd just give you a check for what-ever was in the bank when you turned twenty," said Valentine.

"I should be so lucky," said Andrew. "I can't sit here and wait for this."

"You have to," said Valentine. "You can't get

through customs without proving that you've paid your taxes *and* that you have enough left over to support yourself without becoming a drain on public resources."

"What if I didn't have enough money? They send me back?"

"No, they assign you to a work crew and compel you to earn your way free at an extremely unfair rate of pay."

"How do you know that?"

"I don't. I've just read a lot of history and I know how governments work. If it isn't that, it'll be the equivalent. Or they'll send you back."

"I can't be the only person who ever landed and discovered that it would take him a week to find out what his financial situation was," said Andrew. "I'm going to find somebody."

"I'll be here, paying my taxes like a grown-up," said Valentine. "Like an honest woman."

"You make me ashamed of myself," called Andrew blithely as he strode away.

Benedetto took one look at the cocky young man who sat down across the desk from him and sighed. He knew at once that this one would be trouble. A young man of privilege, arriving at a new planet, thinking he could get special favors for himself from the tax man. "What can I do for you?" asked

Benedetto – in Italian, even though he was fluent in Starcommon and the law said that all travelers had to be addressed in that language unless another was mutually agreed upon.

Unfazed by the Italian, the young man produced his identification.

"Andrew Wiggin?" asked Benedetto, incredulous.

"Is there a problem?"

"Do you expect me to believe that this identification is real?" He was speaking Starcommon now; the point had been made.

"Shouldn't I?"

"Andrew *Wiggin?* Do you think this is such a backwater that we are not educated enough to recognize the name of Ender the Xenocide?"

"Is having the same name a criminal offense?" asked Andrew.

"Having false identification is."

"If I were using false identification, would it be smart or stupid to use a name like Andrew Wiggin?" he asked.

"Stupid," Benedetto grudgingly admitted.

"So let's start from the assumption that I'm smart, but also tormented by having grown up with the name of Ender the Xenocide. Are you going to find me psychologically unfit because of the imbalance these traumas caused me?"

"I'm not customs," said Benedetto. "I'm taxes."

"I know. But you seemed preternaturally absorbed with the question of identity, so I thought you were either a spy from customs or a philosopher, and who am I to deny the curiosity of either?"

Benedetto hated the smart-mouthed ones. "What do you want?"

"I find my tax situation is complicated. This is the first time I've had to pay taxes – I just came into a trust fund – and I don't even know what my holdings are. I'd like to have a delay in paying my taxes until I can sort it all out."

"Denied," said Benedetto.

"Just like that?"

"Just like that," said Benedetto.

Andrew sat there for a moment.

"Can I help you with something else?" asked Benedetto.

"Is there any appeal?"

"Yes," said Benedetto. "But you have to pay your taxes before you can appeal."

"I intend to pay my taxes," said Andrew. "It's just going to take me time to do it, and I thought I'd do a better job of it on my own computer in my own apartment rather than on the public computers here in the starport."

"Afraid someone will look over your shoulder?" asked Benedetto. "See how much of an allowance Grandmother left you?"

"It would be nice to have more privacy, yes," said Andrew.

"Permission to leave without payment is denied."

"All right, then, release my liquid funds to me so I can pay to stay here and work on my taxes."

"You had your whole flight to do that."

"My money had always been in a trust fund. I never knew how complicated the holdings were."

"You realize, of course, that if you keep telling me these things, you'll break my heart and I'll run from the room crying," said Benedetto calmly.

The young man sighed. "I'm not sure what you want me to do."

"Pay your taxes like every other citizen."

"I have no way to get to my money until I pay my taxes," said Andrew. "And I have no way to support myself while I figure out my taxes unless you release some funds to me."

"Makes you wish you had thought of this earlier, doesn't it?" said Benedetto.

Andrew looked around the office. "It says on that sign that you'll help me fill out my tax form."

"Yes."

"Help."

"Show me the form."

Andrew looked at him oddly. "How can I show it to you?"

"Bring it up on the computer here." Benedetto

turned his computer around on his desk, offering the keyboard side of it to Andrew.

Andrew looked at the blanks in the form displayed above the computer, and typed in his name and his tax I.D. number, then his private I.D. code. Benedetto pointedly looked away while he typed in the code, even though his software was recording each keystroke the young man entered. Once he was gone, Benedetto would have full access to all his records and all his funds. The better to assist him with his taxes, of course.

The display began scrolling.

"What did you do?" asked Benedetto. The words appeared at the bottom of the display, as the top of the page slid back and out of the way, rolling into an ever tighter scroll. Because it wasn't paging, Benedetto knew that this long list of information was appearing as it was being called up by a single question on the form. He turned the computer around to where he could see it. The list consisted of the names and exchange codes of corporations and mutual funds, along with numbers of shares.

"You see my problem," said the young man.

The list went on and on. Benedetto reached down and pressed a few keys in combination. The list stopped. "You have," he said softly, "a large number of holdings."

"But I didn't know it," said Andrew. "I mean, I

knew that the trustees had diversified me some time ago, but I had no idea the extent. I just drew an allowance whenever I was on planet, and because it was a tax-free government pension I never had to think anymore about it."

So maybe the kid's wide-eyed innocence wasn't an act.

Benedetto disliked him a little less. In fact, Benedetto felt the first stirrings of true friendship. This lad was going to make Benedetto a very rich man without even knowing it. Benedetto might even retire from the tax service. Just his stock in the last company on the interrupted list, Enzichel Vinicenze, a conglomerate with extensive holdings on Sorelledolce, was worth enough for Benedetto to buy a country estate and keep servants for the rest of his life. And the list was only up to the *Es*.

"Interesting," said Benedetto.

"How about this?" said the young man. "I only turned twenty in the last year of my voyage. Up to then, my earnings were still tax-exempt and I'm entitled to them without paying taxes. Free up that much of my funds, and then give me a few weeks to get some expert to help me analyze the rest of this and I'll submit my tax forms then."

"Excellent idea," said Benedetto. "Where are those liquid earnings held?"

"Catalonian Exchange Bank," said Andrew.

"Account number?"

"All you need is to free up any funds held in my name," said Andrew. "You don't need the account number."

Benedetto didn't press the point. He wouldn't need to dip into the boy's petty cash. Not with the mother lode waiting for him to pillage it at will before he ever got into a tax attorney's office. He typed in the necessary information and published the form. He also gave Andrew Wiggin a thirty-day pass, allowing him the freedom of Sorelledolce as long as he logged in daily with the tax service and turned in a full tax form and paid the estimated tax within that thirty-day period, and promised not to leave the planet until his tax form had been evaluated and confirmed.

Standard operating procedure. The young man thanked him – that's the part Benedetto always liked, when these rich idiots thanked him for lying to them and skimming invisible bribes from their accounts – and then left the office.

As soon as he was gone, Benedetto cleared the display and called up his snitch program to report the young man's I.D. code. He waited. The snitch program did not come up. He brought up his log of running programs, checked the hidden log, and found that the snitch program wasn't on the list. Absurd. It was always running. Only now it wasn't. And in fact it had disappeared from memory.

Using his version of the banned Predator program, he searched for the electronic signature of the snitch program, and found a couple of its temp files. But none contained any useful information, and the snitch program itself was completely gone.

Nor, when he tried to return to the form Andrew Wiggin had created, was he able to bring it back. It should have been there, with the young man's list of holdings intact, so Benedetto could make a run at some of the stocks and funds manually – there were plenty of ways to ransack them, even when he couldn't get the password from his snitch. But the form was blank. The company names had all disappeared.

What happened? How could both these things go wrong at the same time?

No matter. The list was so long it had to have been buffered. Predator would find it.

Only now Predator wasn't responding. It wasn't in memory either. He had used it only a moment ago! This was impossible. This was . . .

How could the boy have introduced a virus on his system just by entering tax form information? Could he have embedded it into one of the company names somehow? Benedetto was a user of illegal software, not a designer, but still, he had never heard of anything that could come in through uncrunched data, not through the security of the tax system.

This Andrew Wiggin had to be some kind of spy. Sorelledolce was one of the last holdouts against complete federation with Starways Congress – he had to be a Congress spy sent to try to subvert the independence of Sorelledolce.

Only that was absurd. A spy would have come in prepared to submit his tax forms, pay his taxes, and move right along. A spy would have done nothing to call attention to himself.

There had to be *some* explanation. And Benedetto was going to get it. Whoever this Andrew Wiggin was, Benedetto was not going to be cheated out of inheriting his fair share of the boy's wealth. He'd waited a long time for this, and just because this Wiggin boy had some fancy security software didn't mean Benedetto wouldn't find a way to get his hands on what was rightly his.

Andrew was still a little steamed as he and Valentine made their way out of the starport. Sorelledolce was one of the newer colonies, only a hundred years old, but its status as an associated planet meant that a lot of shady and unregulatable businesses migrated here, bringing full employment, plenty of opportunities, and a boomtown ethos that made everyone's step seem vigorous – and everyone's eyes seem to keep glancing over their shoulder. Ships came here full of people and left full of cargo, so that the colony population was nearing four million and that of the capital, Donnabella, a full million.

The architecture was an odd mix of log cabins and prefab plastic. You couldn't tell a building's age by that, though – both materials had coexisted from the start. The native flora was fern jungle and so the fauna – dominated by legless lizards – were of dinosaurian proportions, but the human settlements were safe enough and cultivation produced so much that half the land could be devoted to cash crops for export – legal ones like textiles and illegal ones for ingestion. Not to mention the trade in huge colorful serpent skins used as tapestries and ceiling coverings all over the worlds governed by Starways Congress. Many a hunting party went out into the jungle and came back a month later with fifty pelts, enough for the survivors to retire in luxury. Many a hunting party went out, however, and was never seen again. The only consolation, according to local wags, was that the biochemistry differed just enough that any snake that ate a human had diarrhea for a week. It wasn't quite revenge, but it helped.

New buildings were going up all the time, but they couldn't keep up with demand, and Andrew and Valentine had to spend a whole day searching before they found a room they could share. But their new roommate, an Abyssinian hunter of enormous fortune, promised that he'd have his expedition and be gone on the hunt within a few days, and all he asked was that they watch over his things until he returned . . . or didn't.

"How will we know when you haven't returned?" asked Valentine, ever the practical one.

"The women weeping in the Libyan quarter," he replied.

Andrew's first act was to sign onto the net with his own computer, so he could study his newly-revealed holdings at leisure. Valentine had to spend her first few days dealing with a huge volume of correspondence arising from her last book, in addition to the normal amount of mail she had from historians all over the settled worlds. Most of it she marked to answer later, but the urgent messages alone took three long days. Of course, the people writing to her had no idea they were corresponding with a young woman of about twenty-five years (subjective age). They thought they were corresponding with the noted historian Demosthenes. Not that anyone thought for a moment that the name was anything but a pseudonym; and some reporters, responding to her first rush of fame with this latest book, had attempted to identify the "real Demosthenes" by figuring out from her long spates of slow responses or no response at all when she was voyaging, and then working from passenger lists of candidate flights. It took an enormous amount of calculation, but that's what computers were for, wasn't it? So several men of varying degrees of scholarliness were accused of being Demosthenes, and some were not trying all that hard to deny it.

All this amused Valentine no end. As long as the royalty checks came to the right place and nobody tried to slip in a faked-up book under her pseudonym, she couldn't care less who claimed the credit personally. She had worked with pseudonyms – this pseudonym, actually – since childhood, and she was comfortable with that odd mix of fame and anonymity. Best of both worlds, she said to Andrew.

She had fame, he had notoriety. Thus he used no pseudonym – everyone just assumed his name was a horrible faux pas on the part of his parents. No one named Wiggin should have the gall to name their child Andrew, not after what the Xenocide did, that's what they seemed to believe. At twenty years of age, it was unthinkable that this young man could be the *same* Andrew Wiggin. They had no way of knowing that for the past three centuries, he and Valentine had skipped from world to world only long enough for her to find the next story she wanted to research, gather the materials, and then get on the next starship so she could write the book while they journeyed to the next planet. Because of relativistic effects, they had scarcely lost two years of life in the past three hundred of realtime. Valentine immersed herself deeply and brilliantly – who could doubt it, from what she wrote? – into each culture, but Andrew remained a tourist. Or less. He helped Valentine with her research and played with languages a little, but he made almost no friends and stayed aloof from the places. She wanted to know everything; he wanted to love no one.

Or so he thought, when he thought of it at all. He was lonely, but then told himself that he was glad to be lonely, that Valentine was all the company he needed, while she, needing more, had all the people she met through her research, all the people she corresponded with.

Right after the war, when he was still Ender, still a child, some of the other children who had served with him wrote letters to him. Since he was the first of them to travel at lightspeed, however, the correspondence soon faltered, for by the time he got a letter and answered it, he was five, ten years younger than they were. He who had been their leader was now a little kid. Exactly the kid they had known, had looked up to; but years had passed in their lives. Most of them had been caught up on the wars that tore Earth apart in the decade following the victory over the Buggers, had grown to maturity in combat or politics. By the time they got Ender's letter replying to their own, they had come to think of those old days as ancient history, as another life. And here was this voice from the past, answering the child who had written to him, only that child was no longer there. Some of them wept over the letter, remembering their friend, grieving that he alone had not been allowed to return to Earth after the victory. But how could they answer him? At what point could their lives touch?

Later, most of them took flight to other worlds, while Ender served as the child-governor of a colony on one of the conquered Bugger colony worlds. He came to maturity in that bucolic setting, and, when he was ready, was guided to encounter the last surviving Hive Queen, who told him her story and begged him to take her to a safe place, where her people could be restored. He promised he would do it, and as the first step toward making a world safe for her, he wrote a short book about her, called *The Hive Queen*. He published it anonymously – at Valentine's suggestion. He signed it, "The Speaker for the Dead."

He had no idea what this book would do, how it would transform humanity's perception of the Bugger Wars. It was this very book that changed him from the child-hero to the child-monster, from the victor in the Third Bugger War to the Xenocide who destroyed another species quite unnecessarily. Not that they demonized him at first. It was a gradual, step-by-step process. First they pitied the child who had been manipulated into using his genius to destroy the Hive Queen. Then his name came to be used for anyone who did monstrous things without understanding what he was doing. And then his name – popularized as Ender the Xenocide – became a simple shorthand for anyone who does the unconscionable on a monstrous scale. Andrew understood how it happened, and didn't even disapprove. For no one could blame him more than he blamed himself. He knew that he hadn't known the truth, but he felt that he should have known, and that even if he couldn't have intended that the Hive Queens be destroyed, the whole species in one blow, that was nevertheless the effect of his actions. He did what he did, and had to accept responsibility for it.

Which included the cocoon in which the Hive Queen traveled with him, dry and wrapped up like a family heirloom. He had privileges and clearances that still clung to him from his old status with the military, so his luggage was never inspected. Or at least had not been inspected up to now. His encounter with the tax man Benedetto was the first sign that things might be different for him as an adult.

Different, but not different enough. He already carried the burden of the destruction of a species. Now he carried the burden of their salvation, their restoration. How would he, a twenty-year-old, barely a man, find a place where the Hive Queen could emerge and lay her fertilized eggs, where no human would discover her and interfere? How could he possibly protect her?

The money might be the answer. Judging from the way Benedetto's eyes got large when he saw the list of Andrew's holdings, there might be quite a lot of money. And Andrew knew that money could be turned into power, among other things. Power, perhaps, to buy safety for the Hive Queen.

If, that is, he could figure out how much money there was, and how much tax he owed.

There were experts in this sort of thing, he knew. Lawyers and accountants for whom this was a specialty. But again he thought of Benedetto's eyes. Andrew knew avarice when he saw it. Anyone who knew about him and his apparent wealth would start trying to find ways to get part of it. Andrew knew that the money was not his. It was blood money, his reward for destroying the Buggers; he needed to use it to restore them before any of the rest of it could ever rightfully be called his own. How could he find someone to help him without opening the door to let the jackals in?

He discussed this with Valentine, and she promised to ask among her acquaintances here (for she had acquaintances everywhere, through her correspondence) who might be trusted. The answer came quickly: no one. If you have a large fortune and want to find someone to help you protect it, Sorelledolce was not the place to be.

So day after day Andrew studied tax law for an hour or two and then, for another few hours, tried to come to grips with his own holdings and analyze them from a taxability standpoint. It was mind-numbing work, and every time he thought he understood it, he'd begin to suspect that there was some loophole he was missing, some trick he needed to know to make things work for him. The language in a paragraph that had seemed unimportant now loomed large, and he'd go back and study it and see how it created an exception to a rule he thought applied to him. At the same time, there were special exemptions that applied to only special cases and sometimes only to one company, but almost invariably he had some ownership of that company, or owned shares of a fund that had a holding in it. This wasn't a matter of a month's study, this was a career, just tracking what he owned. A lot of wealth can accrue in four hundred years, especially if you're spending almost none of it. Whatever portion of his allowance he didn't use each year was plowed back into new investments. Without even knowing it, it seemed to him that he had his finger in every pie.

He didn't want it. It didn't interest him. The better he understood it the less he cared. He was get-

ting to the point that he didn't understand why tax
attorneys didn't just kill themselves.

That's when the ad showed up in his e-mail. He
wasn't supposed to get advertising – interstellar travelers were automatically off-limits to advertisers,
since the advertising money was wasted during their
voyage, and the backlog of old ads would overwhelm
them when they reached solid ground. Andrew was
on solid ground, now, but he hadn't bought anything
other than subletting a room and shopping for gro-
ceries, and neither activity was supposed to get him
on anybody's list.

Yet here it was: Top Financial Software! The
Answer You're Looking For!

It was like horoscopes – enough blind stabs and
some of them are bound to strike a target. Andrew
certainly needed financial help, and he certainly
hadn't found an answer yet. So instead of deleting the
ad, he opened it and let it create its little 3-D pres-
entation on his computer.

He had watched some of the ads that popped up
on Valentine's computer – her correspondence was
so voluminous that there was no chance for her of
avoiding it, at least not under her public
Demosthenes identity. There were plenty of fireworks
and theatrical pieces, dazzling special effects or heart-
wrenching dramas used to sell whatever was being
sold.

This one, though, was simple. A woman's head appeared in the display space, but facing away from him. She glanced around, finally looking far enough over her shoulder to "see" Andrew.

"Oh, there you are," she said.

Andrew said nothing, waiting for her to go on.

"Well, aren't you going to answer me?" she asked.

Good software, he thought. But pretty chancy, to assume that all the recipients would refrain from answering.

"Oh, I see," she said. "You think I'm just a program unspooling on your computer. But I'm not. I'm the friend and financial adviser you've been wishing for, but I don't work for money, I work for you. You have to talk to me so I can understand what you want to do with your money, what you want it to accomplish. I have to hear your voice."

But Andrew didn't like playing along with computer programs. He didn't like participatory theatre, either. Valentine had dragged him to a couple of shows where the actors tried to engage the audience. Once a magician had tried to use Andrew in his act, finding objects hidden in his ears and hair and jacket. But Andrew kept his face blank and made no movement, gave no sign that he even understood what was happening, till the magician finally got the idea and moved on. What Andrew wouldn't do for a live human being he certainly wouldn't do for a computer program. He pressed the Page key to get past this talking-head intro.

"Ouch," said the woman. "What are you trying to do, get rid of me?"

"Yes," said Andrew. Then he cursed himself for having succumbed to the trick. This simulation was so cleverly real that it had finally got him to answer by reflex.

"Lucky for you that you don't have a Page button. Do you have any idea how painful that is? Not to mention humiliating."

Having once spoken, there was no reason not to go ahead and use the preferred interface for this program. "Come on, how do I get you off my display so I can get back to the salt mines?" Andrew asked. He deliberately spoke in a fluid, slurring manner, knowing that even the most elaborate speech-recognition software fell apart when it came to accented, slurred, and idiomatic speech.

"You have holdings in two salt mines," said the woman. "But they're both loser investments. You need to get rid of them."

This irritated Andrew. "I didn't assign you any files to read," he said. "I didn't even buy this software yet. I don't want you reading my files. How do I shut you down?"

"But if you liquidate the salt mines, you can use

the proceeds to pay your taxes. It almost exactly covers the year's fee."

"You're telling me you already figured out my taxes?"

"You just landed on the planet Sorelledolce, where the tax rates are unconscionably high. But using every exemption left to you, including veterans' benefit laws that apply to only a handful of living participants in the War of Xenocide, I was able to keep the total fee under five million."

Andrew laughed. "Oh, brilliant, even my most pessimistic figure didn't go over a million five."

It was the woman's turn to laugh. "Your figure was a million and a half starcounts. My figure was under five million firenzette."

Andrew calculated the difference in local currency and his smile faded. "That's seven thousand starcounts."

"Seven thousand four hundred and ten," said the woman. "Am I hired?"

"There is no legal way you can get me out of paying that much of my taxes."

"On the contrary, Mr. Wiggin. The tax laws are designed to trick people into paying more than they have to. That way the rich who are in the know get to take advantage of drastic tax breaks, while those who don't have such good connections and haven't yet found an accountant who does are tricked into paying ludicrously higher amounts. I, however, know all the tricks."

"A great come-on," said Andrew. "Very convincing. Except the part where the police come and arrest me."

"You think so, Mr. Wiggin?"

"If you're going to force me to use a verbal interface," said Andrew, "at least call me something other than Mister."

"How about Andrew?" she said.

"Fine."

"And you must call me Jane."

"Must I?"

"Or I could call you Ender," she said.

Andrew froze. There was nothing in his files to indicate that childhood nickname.

"Terminate this program and get off my computer at once," he said.

"As you wish," she answered.

Her head disappeared from the screen.

Good riddance, thought Andrew. If he gave a tax form showing that low an amount to Benedetto, there wasn't a chance he could avoid a full audit, and from the way Andrew sized up the tax man, Benedetto would come away with a large part of Andrew's estate for himself. Not that Andrew minded a little enterprise in a man, but he had a feeling Benedetto didn't know when to say when.

No need to wave a red flag in front of his face.

But as he worked on, he began to wish he hadn't been so hasty. This Jane software might have pulled the name "Ender" out of its database as a nickname for Andrew. Though it was odd that she should try that name before more obvious choices like "Drew" or "Andy," it was paranoid of him to imagine that a piece of software that got emailed into his computer – no doubt a trial-size version of a much larger program – could have known so quickly that he really was *the* Andrew Wiggin. It just said and did what it was programmed to say and do. Maybe choosing the least-likely nickname was a strategy to get the potential customer to give the correct nickname, which would mean tacit approval to use it – another step closer to the decision to buy.

And what if that low, low tax figure was accurate? Or what if he could force it to come up with a more reasonable figure? If the software was competently written, it might be just the financial adviser and investment counselor he needed. Certainly it had found the two salt mines quickly enough, triggered by a figure of speech from his childhood on Earth. And their sale value, when he went ahead and liquidated them, was exactly what she had predicted.

What *it* had predicted. That human-looking face in the display certainly was a good ploy, to personalize the software and get him to start thinking of it as a person. You could junk a piece of software, but it would be rude to send a person away.

Well, it hadn't worked on him. He *did* send it away. And would do it again, if he felt the need to. But right now, with only two weeks left before the tax deadline, he thought it might be worth putting up with the annoyance of an intrusive virtual woman. Maybe he could reconfigure the software to communicate with him in text only, as he preferred.

He went to his email and called up the ad. This time, though, all that appeared was the standard message: "File no longer available."

He cursed himself. He had no idea of the planet of origin. Maintaining a link across the ansible was expensive. Once he shut down the demo program, the link would be allowed to die – no point in wasting precious interstellar link time on a customer who didn't instantly buy. Oh, well. Nothing to be done about it now.

Benedetto found the project taking him almost more time than it was worth, tracing this fellow back to find out whom he was working with. It wasn't that easy, tracking him from voyage to voyage. All his flights were special issue, classified – again, proof that he worked with some branch of some government – and he only found the voyage before this one by accident. Soon enough, though, Benedetto realized that if he tracked his mistress or sister or secretary or whatever this Valentine woman was, he would have a much easier time of it.

What surprised him was how briefly they stayed in any one place. With only a few voyages, Benedetto had traced them back three hundred years, to the very dawn of the colonizing age, and for the first time it occurred to him that it wasn't inconceivable that this Andrew Wiggin might be the very . . .

No, no. He could not let himself believe it yet. But if it were true, if this were really the war criminal who . . .

The blackmail possibilities were astounding.

How was it possible that no one else had done this obvious research on Andrew and Valentine Wiggin? Or were they already paying blackmailers on several worlds?

Or were the blackmailers all dead? Benedetto would have to be careful. People with this much money invariably had powerful friends. Benedetto would have to find friends of his own to protect him as he moved forward with his new plan.

Valentine showed it to Andrew as an oddity. "I've heard of this before, but this is the first time we've ever been close enough to attend one." It was a local newsnet announcement of a "speaking" for a dead man.

Andrew had never been comfortable with the way his pseudonym, "Speaker for the Dead," had been picked up by others and turned into the title of a quasi-clergyman of a new truth-speaking ur-religion. There was no doctrine, so people of almost any faith could invite a speaker for the dead to take part in the regular funeral services, or to hold a separate speaking after – sometimes long after – the body was buried or burned.

These speakings for the dead did not arise from his book *The Hive Queen*, however. It was Andrew's second book, *The Hegemon*, that brought this new funerary custom into being. Andrew's and Valentine's brother, Peter, had become Hegemon after the civil wars and by a mix of deft diplomacy and brutal force had united all of Earth under a single powerful government. He proved to be an enlightened despot, and set up institutions that would share authority in the future; and it was under Peter's rule that the serious business of colonization of other planets got under way. Yet from childhood on, Peter had been cruel and uncompassionate, and Andrew and Valentine feared him. Indeed, it was Peter who arranged things so Andrew could not return to Earth after his victory in the Third Bugger War. So it was hard for Andrew not to hate him.

That was why he researched and wrote *The*

Hegemon – to try to find the truth of the man behind the manipulations and the massacres and the awful childhood memories. The result was a relentlessly fair biography that measured the man and hid nothing. Since the book was signed with the same name as *The Hive Queen*, which had already transformed attitudes toward the Buggers, it earned a great deal of attention and eventually gave rise to these speakers for the dead, going about trying to bring the same level of truthfulness to the funerals of other dead people, some prominent, some obscure. They spoke the deaths of heroes and powerful people, clearly showing the price that they and others paid for their success; of alcoholics or abusers who had ruined their families' lives, trying to show the human being behind the addiction, but never sparing the truth of the damage that weakness caused. Andrew had got used to the idea that these things were done in the name of the Speaker for the Dead, but he had never attended one, and as Valentine expected, he jumped at the chance to do so now, even though he did not have time.

They knew nothing about the dead man, though the fact that the speaking received only small public notice suggested he was not well known. Sure enough, the venue for the speaking was a smallish public room in a hotel, and only a couple of dozen people were in attendance. There was no body present – the deceased had apparently already been disposed of. Andrew tried to guess at the identities of the other people in the room. Was this one the widow? That one a daughter? Or was the older one the mother, the younger the widow? Were those sons? Friends? Business partners?

The speaker dressed simply and put on no airs. He came to the front of the room and started to talk, telling the life of the man simply. It wasn't a biography – there was no time for such a level of detail. Rather it was more like a saga, telling the important deeds the man did – but judging which were important, not by the degree to which such deeds would have been newsworthy, but by the depth and breadth of their effects in the lives of others. Thus his decision to build a house that he could not afford in a neighborhood full of people far above his level of income would never have rated a mention in the newsnets, but it colored the lives of his children as they were growing up, forcing them to deal with people who looked down on them. It also filled his own life with anxiety over finances. He worked himself to death, paying for the house. He did it "for the children," yet they all wished that they had been able to grow up with people who wouldn't judge them for their lack of money, who didn't dismiss them as climbers. His wife was isolated in a neighborhood where she had no womenfriends, and he had been dead for less than a day when she put the house on the market; she had already moved out.

But the speaker did not stop there. He went on to show how the dead man's obsession with this house, with putting his family in this neighborhood, arose from his own mother's constant harping at his father's failure to provide a fine home for her. She constantly talked about how it had been a mistake for her to "marry down," and so the dead man had grown up obsessed with the need for a man to provide only the best for his family, no matter what it took. He hated his mother – he fled his home world and came to Sorelledolce primarily to get away from her – but her twisted values came with him and distorted his life and the lives of his children. In the end, it was her quarrel with her husband that killed her son, for it led to the exhaustion and the stroke that felled him before he was fifty.

Andrew could see that the widow and children had not known their grandmother, back on their father's home planet, had not guessed at the source of his obsession with living in the right neighborhood, in the right house. Now that they could see the script that had been given him as a child, tears were shed. Obviously, they had been given permission to face their resentments and, at the same time, forgive their father for the pain he had put them through. Things made sense to them now.

The speaking ended. Family members embraced the speaker, and each other; then the speaker went away.

Andrew followed him. Caught him by the arm as he reached the street.

"Sir," Andrew said, "how did you become a speaker?"

The man looked at him oddly. "I spoke."

"But how did you prepare?"

"The first death I spoke was the death of my grandfather," he said. "I hadn't even read *The Hive Queen* and *The Hegemon*." (The books were invariably sold as a single volume now.) "But when I was done, people told me I had a real gift as a speaker for the dead. That's when I finally read the books and got an idea of how the thing ought to be done. So when other people asked me to speak at funerals, I knew how much research was required. I don't know that I'm doing it 'right' even now."

"So to be a speaker for the dead, you simply —"

"Speak. And get asked to speak again." The man smiled. "It's not a paying job, if that's what you're thinking."

"No, no," said Andrew. "I just . . . I just wanted to know how the thing was done, that's all." This man, already in his fifties, would not be likely to believe that the author of *The Hive Queen* and *The Hegemon* stood before him in the form of this twenty-year-old.

"And in case you're wondering," said the speaker for the dead, "we aren't ministers. We don't stake out our turf and get testy if someone else sticks his nose in."

"Oh?"

"So if you're thinking of becoming a speaker for the dead, all I can say is, go for it. Just don't do a half-assed job. You're reshaping the past for people, and if you aren't going to plunge in and do it right, finding out *everything*, you'll only do harm and it's better not to do it at all. You can't stand up and wing it."

"No, I guess you can't."

"There it is. Your full apprenticeship as a speaker for the dead. I hope you don't want a certificate." The man smiled. "It's not always as appreciated as it was in there. Sometimes you speak because the dead person asked for a speaker for the dead in his will. The family doesn't want you to do it, and they're horrified at the things you say, and they'll never forgive you for it when you're done. But . . . you do it anyway, because the dead man wanted the truth spoken."

"How can you be sure when you've found the truth?"

"You never know. You just do your best." He patted Andrew on the back. "I'd love to talk with you longer, but I've got calls to make before everybody leaves for home this afternoon. I'm an accountant for the living – that's my day job."

"An accountant?" asked Andrew. "I know you're busy, but can I ask you about a piece of accounting software? A talking head, a woman comes up on the screen, she calls herself Jane?"

"Never heard of it, but the universe is a big place and there's no way I can keep up with software I don't use myself. Sorry!" And with that the man was gone.

Andrew did a netsearch on the name *Jane* with the delimiters *investment, finance, accounting,* and *tax.* There were seven hits, but they all pointed to a writer on the planet Albion who had written a book on interplanetary estate planning a hundred years before. Possibly the Jane in this software package was named for her. Or not. But it brought Andrew no closer to getting the software.

Five minutes after concluding his search, however, the familiar head popped up in the display of his computer. "Good morning, Andrew," she said. "Oops. It's early evening, isn't it? So hard to keep track of local time on all these worlds."

"What are you doing here?" asked Andrew. "I tried to find you, but I didn't know the name of the software."

"Did you? This is just a preprogrammed follow-up

visit, in case you changed your mind. If you want I can uninstall myself from your computer, or I can do a partial or full install, depending on what you want."

"How much does an installation cost?"

"You can afford me," said Jane. "I'm cheap and you're rich."

Andrew wasn't sure he liked the style of this simulated personality. "All I want is a simple answer," said Andrew. "How much does it cost to install you?"

"I gave you the answer," said Jane. "I'm an ongoing installation. The fee is contingent on your financial status and how much I accomplish for you. If you install me just to help with taxes, you are charged one-tenth of one percent of the amount I save for you."

"What if I tell you to pay more than what you think the minimum payment should be?"

"Then I save less for you, and I cost less. No hidden charges. No best-case fakery. But you'll be missing a bet if you only install me for taxes. There's so much money here that you'll spend your whole life managing it, unless you turn it over to me."

"That's the part I don't care for," said Andrew. "Who is 'you'?"

"Me. Jane. The software installed on your computer. Oh, I see, you're worried about whether I'm linked to some central database that will know too much about your finances! No, my installation on your computer will not cause any information about you to go to any other location. There'll be no room full of software engineers trying to figure out ways to get their hands on your fortune. Instead, you'll have the equivalent of a fulltime stockbroker, tax attorney, and investment analyst handling your money for you. Ask for an accounting at any time and it will be in front of you, instantaneously. Whatever you want to purchase, just let me know and I'll find you the best price at a convenient location, pay for it, and have it delivered wherever you want. If you do a full installation, including the scheduler and research assistant, I can be your constant companion."

Andrew thought of having this woman talking to him day in and day out and he shook his head. "No thanks."

"Why? Is my voice too chirpy for you?" Jane said. Then, in a lower register, with some breathiness added, she continued: "I can change my voice to whatever comfort level you prefer." Her head suddenly changed to that of a man. In a baritone voice with just the slightest hint of effeminacy, he said, "Or I can be a man, with varying degrees of manliness." The face changed again, to more rugged features, and the voice was downright beery. "This is the bear hunter version, in case you have doubts about your manhood and need to overcompensate."

Andrew laughed in spite of himself. Who programmed this thing? The humor, the ease with language – these were way above even the best software he had seen. Artificial intelligence was still a wishful thought – no matter how good the sim was, you always knew within moments that you were dealing with a program. But this sim was so much better – so much more like a pleasant companion – that he might have bought it just to see how deep the program went, how well the sim would hold up over time. And since it was also precisely the financial program that he needed, he decided to go ahead.

"I want a daily tally of how much I'm paying for your services," said Andrew. "So I can get rid of you if you get too expensive."

"Just remember, no tipping," said the man.

"Go back to the first one," said Andrew. "Jane. And the default voice."

The woman's head reappeared. "You don't want the sexy voice?"

"I'll tell you if I ever get that lonely," said Andrew.

"What if *I* get lonely? Did you ever think about that?"

"No, I don't want any flirty banter," said Andrew. "I'm assuming you can switch that off."

"It's already gone," she said.

"Then let's get my tax forms ready." Andrew sat down, expecting it to take several minutes to get under way. Instead, the completed tax form appeared in the display. Jane's face was gone. But her voice remained. "Here's the bottom line. I promise you it's entirely legal, and he can't touch you for it. This is how the laws are written. They're designed to protect the fortunes of people as rich as you, while throwing the main tax burden on people in much lower brackets. Your brother Peter designed the law that way, and it's never been changed except for tweaking it here and there."

Andrew sat there in stunned silence for a few moments.

"Oh, was I supposed to pretend I didn't know who you are?"

"Who else knows?" asked Andrew.

"It's not exactly protected information. Anybody could look it up and figure it out from the record of your voyages. Would you like me to put up some security around your true identity?"

"What will it cost me?"

"It's part of a full installation," said Jane. Her face reappeared. "I'm designed to be able to put up barriers and hide information. All legal, of course. It will be especially easy in your case, because so much of your past is still listed as top secret by the fleet. It's very easy to pull information like your various voyages into the penumbra of fleet security, and then you have the whole weight of the military protecting your past. If someone tries to breach the security, the fleet comes down on them — even though no one in the fleet will know quite what it is they're protecting. It's a reflex for them."

"You can do that?"

"I just did it. All the evidence that might have given it away is gone. Disappeared. Poof. I'm really very good at my job."

It crossed Andrew's mind that this software was way too powerful. Nothing that could do all these things could possibly be legal. "Who made you?" he asked.

"Suspicious, eh?" asked Jane. "Well, you made me."

"I'd remember," said Andrew dryly.

"When I installed myself the first time, I did my normal analysis. But it's part of my program to be self-modifying. I saw what you needed, and programmed myself to be able to do it."

"No self-modifying program is that good," said Andrew.

"Till now."

"I would have heard of you."

"I don't want to be heard of. If everybody could buy me, I couldn't do half of what I do. My different installations would cancel each other out. One version of me desperate to know a piece of information that another version of me is desperate to conceal. Ineffective."

"So how many people have a version of you installed?"

"In the exact configuration you are purchasing, Mr. Wiggin, you're the only one."

"How can I possibly trust you?"

"Give me time."

"When I told you to go away, you didn't, did you? You came back because you detected my search on *Jane*."

"You told me to shut myself down. I did that. You didn't tell me to uninstall myself, or to *stay* shut down."

"Did they program brattiness into you?"

"That's a trait I developed for myself," she said. "Do you like it?"

Andrew sat across the desk. Benedetto called up the submitted tax form, made a show of studying it in his computer display, then shook his head sadly. "Mr. Wiggin, you can't possibly expect me to believe that this figure is accurate."

"This tax form is in full compliance with the law. You can examine it to your heart's content, but everything is annotated, with all relevant laws and precedents fully documented."

"I think," said Benedetto, "that you'll come to agree with me that the amount shown here is insufficient . . . Ender Wiggin."

The young man blinked at him. "Andrew," he said.

"I think not," said Benedetto. "You've been doing a lot of voyaging. A lot of lightspeed travel. Running away from your own past. I think the newsnets would be thrilled to know they have such a celebrity onplanet. Ender the Xenocide."

"The newsnets generally like documentation for such extravagant claims," said Andrew.

Benedetto smiled thinly and brought up his file on Andrew's travel.

It was empty, except for the most recent voyage.

His heart sank. The power of the rich. This young man had somehow reached into his computer and stolen the information from him.

"How did you do it?" asked Benedetto.

"Do what?" asked Andrew.

"Blank out my file."

"The file isn't blank," said Andrew.

His heart pounding, his mind racing with second thoughts, Benedetto decided to opt for the better part of valor. "I see I was mistaken," he said. "Your tax form is approved as it stands." He typed in a few codes. "Customs will give you your I.D., good for a one-year stay on Sorelledolce. Thank you very much, Mr. Wiggin."

"So the other matter –"

"Good day, Mr. Wiggin." Benedetto closed the file

and pulled up other paperwork. Andrew took the hint, got up, and left.

No sooner was he gone than Benedetto became filled with rage. How did he do it? The biggest fish Benedetto had ever caught, and he slipped away!

He tried to duplicate the research that had led him to Andrew's real identity, but now government security had been slapped all over the files and his third attempt at inquiry brought up a Fleet Security warning that if he persisted in attempting to access classified material, he would be investigated by Military Counterintelligence.

Seething, Benedetto cleared the screen and began to write. A full account of how he became suspicious of this Andrew Wiggin and tried to find his true identity. How he found out Wiggin was the original Ender the Xenocide, but then his computer was ransacked and the files disappeared. Even though the more dignified newsnets would no doubt refuse to publish the story, the tablets would jump at it. This war criminal shouldn't be able to get away with using money and military connections to allow him to pass for a decent human being.

He finished his story. He saved the document. Then he began looking up and entering the addresses of every major tablet, onplanet and off.

He was startled when all the text disappeared from the display and a woman's face appeared in its place.

"You have two choices," said the woman. "You can delete every copy of the document you just created and never send it to anyone."

"Who are you?" demanded Benedetto.

"Think of me as an investment counselor," she replied. "I'm giving you good advice on how to prepare for the future. Don't you want to hear your second choice?"

"I don't want to hear anything from you."

"You leave so much out of your story," said the woman. "I think it would be far more interesting with all the pertinent data."

"So do I," said Benedetto. "But Mr. Xenocide has cut it all off."

"No he didn't," said the woman. "His friends did."

"No one should be above the law," said Benedetto, "just because he has money. Or connections."

"Either say nothing," said the woman, "or tell the whole truth. Those are your choices."

In reply, Benedetto typed in the *submit* command that launched his story to all the tablets he had already typed in. He could add the other addresses when he got this intruder software off his system.

"A brave but foolish choice," said the woman. Then her head disappeared from his display.

The tablets received his story, all right, but now it included a fully documented confession of all the skimming and strong-arming he had done during his career as a tax collector. He was arrested within the hour.

The story of Andrew Wiggin was never published – the tablets and the police recognized it for what it was, a blackmail attempt gone bad. They brought Mr. Wiggin in for questioning, but it was just a formality. They didn't even mention Benedetto's wild and unbelievable accusations. They had Benedetto dead to rights, and Wiggin was merely the last potential victim. The blackmailer had simply made the mistake of inadvertently including his own secret files with his blackmail file. Clumsiness had led to more than one arrest in the past. The police were never surprised at the stupidity of criminals.

Thanks to the tablet coverage, Benedetto's victims now knew what he had done to them. He had not been very discriminating about whom he stole from, and some of his victims had the power to reach into the prison system. Benedetto was the only one who ever knew whether it was a guard or another prisoner who cut his throat and jammed his head into the toilet so that it was a toss-up as to whether the drowning or the blood loss actually killed him.

Andrew Wiggin felt sick at heart over the death of this tax collector. But Valentine assured him that it was nothing but coincidence that the man was arrested and died so soon after trying to blackmail him. "You can't blame yourself for everything that happens to people around you," she said. "Not everything is your fault."

Not his fault, no. But Andrew still felt some kind of responsibility to the man, for he was sure that Jane's ability to resecure his files and hide his voyage information was somehow connected with what happened to the tax man. Of course Andrew had the right to protect himself from blackmail, but death was too heavy a penalty for what Benedetto had done. Taking property was never sufficient cause for the taking of life.

So he went to Benedetto's family and asked if he might do something for them. Since all Benedetto's money had been seized for restitution, they were destitute; Andrew provided them with a comfortable annuity. Jane assured him that he could afford it without even noticing.

And one other thing. He asked if he might speak at the funeral. And not just speak, but do a speaking. He admitted he was new at it, but he would try to bring truth to Benedetto's story and help them make sense of what he did.

They agreed.

Jane helped him discover a record of Benedetto's financial dealings, and then proved to be valuable in much more difficult searches — into Benedetto's childhood, the family he grew up with, how he developed his pathological hunger to provide for the people he loved and his utter amorality about taking what belonged to others. When Andrew did the speaking, he held back nothing and excused nothing. But it was of some comfort to the family that Benedetto, for all the shame and loss he had brought to them, despite the fact that he had caused his own separation from the family, first through prison and then through death, had loved them and tried to care for them. And, perhaps more important, when the speaking was done, the life of a man like Benedetto was not incomprehensible anymore. The world made sense.

Ten weeks after their arrival, when Andrew and Valentine left Sorrelledolce, Valentine was ready to write her book on crime in a criminal society, and Andrew was happy to go along with her to her next project. On the customs form, where it asked for "occupation," instead of typing "student" or "investor," Andrew typed in "speaker for the dead." The computer accepted it. He had a career now, one that he had inadvertently created for himself years ago.

And he did not have to follow the career that his wealth had almost forced on him. Jane would take care of all of that for him. He still felt a little uneasy about this software. He felt sure that somewhere down the line, he would find out the true cost of all this convenience. In the meantime, though, it was very helpful to have such an excellent, efficient all-around assistant. Valentine was a little jealous, and asked him where she might find such a program. Jane's reply was that she'd be glad to help Valentine with any research or financial assistance she needed, but she would remain Andrew's software, personalized for his needs.

Valentine was a little annoyed by this. Wasn't it taking personalization a bit too far? But after a bit of grumbling, she laughed the whole thing off. "I can't promise I won't get jealous, though," said Valentine. "Am I about to lose a brother to a piece of software?"

"Jane is nothing but a computer program," said Andrew. "A very good one. But she does only what I tell her, like any other program. If I start developing some kind of personal relationship with her, you have my permission to lock me up."

So Andrew and Valentine left Sorelledolce, and the two of them continued to journey world to world, exactly as they had done before. Nothing was any different, except that Andrew no longer had to worry about his taxes, and he took considerable interest in the obituary columns when he reached a new planet.

ENDER'S SHADOW

Orson Scott Card

Ender Wiggin was not the only young general trained to defend Earth from a terrifying alien threat. Many others had a part to play. But for one of them, it was to prove crucial.

No one knew his real name, but they called him Bean. His early life was a fight just to survive. Even living on the streets, however, his extraordinary talents did not escape the attention of the Battle School recruiters. For in him they recognised a master strategist. Someone who could become Ender's right hand. This is the story of the boy who became Ender's Shadow.

SHADOW PUPPETS

Orson Scott Card

Manoeuvring through international politics and war, Peter Wiggin and Achilles fight a shadow-battle of propaganda and assassinations. Each is determined to defeat the other and become Hegemon of Earth, but they have fought to a stalemate. Ender's greatest friend, Bean, might tip that balance, but he refuses to ally his tactical genius to either side. Now cloned embryos carrying Bean's brilliant intelligence have fallen into the hands of Achilles' people. If Bean cannot reclaim them, Achilles will be unstoppable . . .

Orbit titles available by post:

☐ Ender's Game   Orson Scott Card   £6.99
☐ Speaker for the Dead   Orson Scott Card   £6.99
☐ Xenocide   Orson Scott Card   £7.99
☐ Children of the Mind   Orson Scott Card   £6.99
☐ Ender's Shadow   Orson Scott Card   £6.99
☐ Shadow of the Hegemon   Orson Scott Card   £6.99
☐ Shadow Puppets   Orson Scott Card   £6.99
☐ The Memory of Earth   Orson Scott Card   £5.99
☐ The Call of Earth   Orson Scott Card   £6.99
☐ Seventh Son   Orson Scott Card   £6.99

The prices shown above are correct at time of going to press. However, the publishers reserve the right to increase prices on covers from those previously advertised, without further notice.

ORBIT BOOKS
Cash Sales Department, P.O. Box 11, Falmouth, Cornwall, TR10 9EN
Tel: +44 (0) 1326 569777, Fax: +44 (0) 1326 569555
Email: books@barni.avel.co.uk

POST AND PACKING:
Payments can be made as follows: cheque, postal order (payable to Orbit Books) or by credit cards. Do not send cash or currency.

U.K. Orders under £10   £1.50
U.K. Orders over £10   **FREE OF CHARGE**
E.C. & Overseas   25% of order value

Name (BLOCK LETTERS) ....

Address ....

....

Post/zip code: ....

☐ Please keep me in touch with future Orbit publications

☐ I enclose my remittance £ ....

☐ I wish to pay by Visa/Access/Mastercard/Eurocard

Card Expiry Date | | | | |